Hann
you li
tric
like the terrible-2
of Tin City.
Enjoy,
Cousin Rob.

Order this book online at www.trafford.com/07-0237
or email orders@trafford.com

Most Trafford titles are also available at major online book retailers.

Note for Librarians: A cataloguing record for this book is available from Library
and Archives Canada at www.collectionscanada.ca/amicus/index-e.html

Printed in Victoria, BC, Canada.

ISBN: 978-1-4251-1827-3

*We at Trafford believe that it is the responsibility of us all, as both individuals
and corporations, to make choices that are environmentally and socially sound.
You, in turn, are supporting this responsible conduct each time you purchase a
Trafford book, or make use of our publishing services. To find out how you are
helping, please visit www.trafford.com/responsiblepublishing.html*

*Our mission is to efficiently provide the world's finest, most comprehensive
book publishing service, enabling every author to experience success.
To find out how to publish your book, your way, and have it available
worldwide, visit us online at www.trafford.com/10510*

**TrafFord**
PUBLISHING™

www.trafford.com

**North America & international**
toll-free: 1 888 232 4444 (USA & Canada)
phone: 250 383 6864 ♦ fax: 250 383 6804
email: info@trafford.com

**The United Kingdom & Europe**
phone: +44 (0)1865 722 113 ♦ local rate: 0845 230 9601
facsimile: +44 (0)1865 722 868 ♦ email: info.uk@trafford.com

10 9 8 7 6 5 4 3 2

This book is dedicated to the students at Middlebury Public School. To the hundreds of boys and girls who listened, laughed, and drew pictures. To the kids who wrote their own 'Meaner Beaner' stories and shared them with their 'reading buddies.' And to all the story-lovers who thought of new ideas, new capers, and made important suggestions to the author. Middlebury Public School rocks!

Special thanks to Heather for your hours of proof reading. As a good nurse you have helped this book to get a lot better.
**Robert Harry Kerr – who wrote every word**

For my younger brother, Peter, who insisted I tell him a story every night.
**Rick Taylor – who drew every picture**

# Contents

Meet the 'Terrible Two'

1  The Meaner Beaner Ruins Valentine's Day

2  Pet Day

3  The Super Sleepover

4  The Meaner Takes the Test of the Three Skulls

5  The Meaner Beaner Skips School

6  Joy Ride

7  The New Neighbor

8  The P...P...Pool Party

9  The Trip to New Zoo

10  The Big Game

11  The Headless Horseman of Tin City

12  The Meaner Beaner Steals Christmas

# Meet the 'Terrible Two'

Meet William Joseph Beaner. He is unlike anyone else in Tin City, Ohio. In fact, he is unlike any other kid on the planet, Earth.

William Joseph Beaner is the meanest kid on the block. He lives inside the house of 11 Brick Street. He's the kid with the pinched face, green flinty eyes, and the slithery smile of a garter snake. He has a soup-bowl haircut—"warm on top, cool on the sides," he likes to tell the other kids. He loves this haircut, he tells them, "because all the girls hate it." Today he is wearing the shirt with the green-skinned zombie on front. Yesterday, it was the shirt with the lop-eared ghoul, and on Thursday it was the shirt with the skull and crossbones. This boy chooses shirts that scare the kindergarten kids. The kids don't call him William or Willy or Billy or Joseph or Joe, no, no, no.

They call him the Meaner Beaner.

Meet Rat Zakary. The Meaner's one true friend in the world. Zakary lives in a wire cage in the Meaner's bedroom. He has fiery red eyes, razor-sharp claws and a tail as long as a shoe string.

The boy and the rat walk down the steps, into their dark basement. They make their way to a dark corner, where one lonely light bulb keeps the room from complete blackness. This is their favorite spot in the whole world, and the big box in front of them is their favorite thing in the whole world. Words are painted on the side: **Secret Box of No-Good Dirty Rotten Tricks.** The lid of the box is raised. The human and the rat look happily down to the collection of gruesome goodies: the goo gun, the tin can of slimy worms, jars of black spiders, stink bombs, exploding ink pens, plastic barf, firecrackers, red paint, rubber snakes, gory masks, coyote teeth, axle grease, sharp tacks, a pea shooter, strings, rotten apples, goose feathers. These things are their treasures. Things that bring them great happiness.

Things that can ruin the parties and picnics and plans of those goodie-goodie Brick Street kids.

The boy looks at the rat: "You are my buddy until the end of time," he tells the rat. "But those goodie-goodie Brickstreeters will be our mortal enemies. We will caper them every day. We will caper them real good. We will ruin their parties. We will spoil their fun. We will come into their night-time dreams with masks and snakes and scary, scary things. We will be their worst nightmare. This will be our mission in life."

Nyuk, nyuk, nyuk, goes the boy. Chidder, chidder, chidder, goes the rat.

Then, from the bottom of the **Secret Box of No-Good Dirty Rotten Tricks**, the Meaner lifts a sheet of paper. This is their secret Caper Creed. The creed that tells their mission in life. The boy stands tall and puts one hand over his heart. The rat sits up tall and puts one claw over its heart. Then, under the dim light bulb, the Meaner Beaner reads their secret Caper Creed.

A caper is a beautiful thing,
Grease on a swing,
Slime on a ring,
A tricky trick, a pranky prank,
A ring-a-ding-ding.

Oh, to ruin their day,
To stifle their play.

Dip their schoolbooks in oily oil,
Bury their gumdrops in soily soil,
And yes, oh yes—all their birthdays we plan to foil!
Don't like it much when a birdie sings,
Don't like it much when the school bell dings,
But capering, capering, capering,
Capering is such a beautiful thing!

Those missing toys they'll never find,
That sticky gum on their behinds,
Here it comes, you better duck,
One more caper is your bad luck,
Chidder, chidder, chidder and nyuk, nyuk, nyuk.

Oh, those Goodie-Goodies!
They'll forget the history they learned in school,
They'll forget if the day was hot or cool,
But our capers most terrible, dirty and rotten,
These for sure will NOT be forgotten.
The picnic is right for Zakary and me,
If there's a caper or two or twenty-three.
Drop a snake in some hoodies,
Make a stain, cause some pain,
For those soft-bellied Goodie-Goodies.

A stink-bug here, a garter snake there,
Red ants in their soup and their underwear.
Bug the babysitter,
Make her soft drink bitter,
Nyuk, nyuk, nyuk and chidder, chidder, chidder.

Let the Goodies have their good,
Let the Goodies do as they should.

Rotten capers is all we see,
Rotten capers they'll get for free.
And BAD—that's good enough for Zakary and me!
A caper is a beautiful thing,
A tricky trick, a pranky prank,
And a ring-a-ding-ding.

# Chapter One

## The Meaner Beaner Ruins Valentine's Day

It was Thursday, February 13. The sky was as bleak and colorless as a chalkboard and the sidewalk was cold and slushy. No matter. The kids on Brick Street tramped along with sunny smiles. On this cool day their hearts were warm. Tomorrow would be special—their teachers told them so—a day for trading paper hearts and wishing happy wishes and eating chocolate candies. The kids in Ms. Barnyard's class were especially happy, for tomorrow they would have their Valentine's Day party.

William Joseph Beaner HATED Valentine's Day. He HATED those mushy red cards kids gave to each other every February 14. He HATED Valentine's Day parties. Most of all, he HATED when other kids had fun. In fact, KIDS HAVING FUN was his worst nightmare.

No doubt about it—William Joseph Beaner was the meanest kid on Brick Street. He was the meanest kid in Brick Street School. And of all the kids who cut through Brick Street Park, there was no one meaner. He was meaner than a pinching bug, meaner than a hissing cat. That's why the kids called him the Meaner Beaner. The Meaner loved that.

The Brickstreeters were full of excitement. Just past the crosswalk Sadie Orson and Frannie O'Neill caught up to the Meaner. "Hey, Meaner, said Frannie, "you are going to LOVE the green cake I am bringing to the party tomorrow. And Sadie is bringing a zillion of those red-hot candy hearts. It's going to be the BEST PARTY IN THE HISOTRY OF BRICK STREET SCHOOL!"

The Meaner gave the girls a vinegary scowl.

1

"VALENTINE'S DAY IS FOR PINHEADS." The girls simply smiled and shrugged and skipped along. The Meaner was always like that. Frannie thought he was probably hatched from an egg. She had heard that on the day he was hatched, the Meaner baby kicked the doctor in the stomach.

Little Mouse Krause came walking the other way, her brown wiener dog on a long leash, and her pigtails bouncing as she jumped the slush puddles. Mouse Krause was the littlest kid in Meaner's class, 59 pounds soaking wet. "Hi, Meaner," she said cheerily. "Are you excited about tomorrow's party? I'm bringing jelly-jam sandwiches. You're going to LOVE them."

The Meaner gave the wiener dog his meanest glare. "That dog looks like a giant fish worm." The wiener dog growled at Meaner, and the Meaner growled back.

Mouse Krause whispered to her long dog: "It's okay, Digger, it's just the Meaner Beaner. He growls but he won't bite you. Frannie O'Neill thinks he was born like that." Mouse pulled Digger's leash and moved along. "See you Meaner," she said brightly.

When the Meaner Beaner reached 11 Brick Street, he opened the door and dropped his school bag on the floor. A sweet voice greeted him from the kitchen: "Is that you, dear?"

"Yes, Mummy," said the Meaner, nice as pie. "Guess what, Mummy? Ms. Barnyard is letting us have a Valentine's Day party tomorrow, and I would like to bring some treats for all the kids."

"Oh, that's so very nice, dear. You are such a wonderful, thoughtful boy. If you go upstairs and write your valentines, I will bake some fudge brownies for the whole class. When your father gets home we will have our supper."

The Meaner went up the stairs and shut his bedroom door. He went over to the cage of his one true friend, Rat Zakary. "We have a SSSSSTUPID, NO-GOOD Valentine's Day party tomorrow, Zakary. VALENTINES ARE FOR PINHEADS." Zakary was munching on a monarch butterfly. The pet had cocoa-brown fur, a long snake-like tail, bright red eyes, razor-sharp fangs, needle-sharp claws, and an evil smile on its furry face.

Zakary liked mean kids. He loved the Meaner Beaner.

After supper the Meaner's mom made some delicious chocolate fudge for tomorrow's party, enough for everybody in the class. When she was not looking, the Meaner took five brownies and ate them up in his bedroom.

That night the Meaner Beaner could hardly sleep. His night was filled with horrible dreams of kids eating chocolate brownies and trading paper hearts and having fun. He squirmed in his bed, and tossed and turned. And then, a strange, magical thing happened. An evil idea smoldered up from the rat's brain, like a puff of black smoke, and it sailed across the dark bedroom and landed softly on the Meaner's sleeping brain. The Meaner had been ZAPPED.

Suddenly the Meaner awoke. He got out of bed and walked over to the wire cage, picked up the rat, and kissed him on the whiskers. "Thank you, thank you, little friend. You have zapped me with a wonderful, wonderful, rotten dream: "Tomorrow, I am going to caper those goodie-goodies at Brick Street School. I am going to ruin Valentine's Day." Nyuk, nyuk, nyuk, went the Meaner Beaner. Chidder, chidder, chidder went Rat Zakary

The Meaner went over to his desk and flicked on the light. "It's time to write some Meaner Beaner valentines," he said to Zakary, and he began to write. For two hours the Meaner wrote valentines, hundreds of them, reading each of them to Zakary as they were done, and the two of them snickered and chiddered in the dim room.

Then, as quiet as midnight, the Meaner sneaked downstairs and into the kitchen. His meaner heart was filled with glee. He snapped on the counter light and noticed Mom's chocolate brownies. He began eating the brownies as he made up his own special treats for tomorrow's party.

"What this party needs are some Meaner Beaner sandwiches," he muttered to himself. He set out two loaves of bread, neatly buttered each slice, and prepared them for the delicious filling. From the cupboard he opened three cans of Frisky Cat Food, spread it on the slices of bread, and the Meaner grinned his meanest grin. "Wait 'til those goodie-goodies taste the MEANER'S CAT FOOD SANDWICHES." Nyuk, nyuk, nyuk.

"Now, for some tasty fruit punch to wash it down," he chuckled. From Mom's pantry the Meaner chose one can of orange juice, one can of cranberry juice, two cans of apple juice—and four huge jars of sour vinegar. Mixing the drinks together, the Meaner Beaner could hardly keep from laughing. "Wait 'til those goodie-goodies drink some MEANER BEANER VINEGAR PUNCH." Nyuk, nyuk, nyuk.

"Everybody likes creamy cookies," he giggled. From the cupboard the trickster snatched a large bag of Creamo Cream-Filled Cookies. He pried the two ends of each cookie apart and scraped away the creamy filling. He then spread his own cream filling onto the cookies—Dr. John's Shiny White Shoe Polish—and put the ends together. The Meaner's black heart was pounding with excitement. "Wait 'til those goodie-goodies munch on the MEANER'S SHOE POLISH COOKIES." Nyuk, nyuk, nyuk.

"And finally," the Meaner whispered to himself, "there is always room for strawberry Jell-O." Just like he had seen his mom do hundreds of times, the Meaner mixed strawberry Jell-O powder with hot water in a giant bowl.

He then ran down to the basement, opened his **Secret Box of No-Good Dirty Rotten Tricks** and returned with an old tin can. Out of the can he scooped the final ingredients for his Jell-O dessert—two hundred red ants. He finished off the last of Mom's brownies and smiled his meanest smile. "Wait 'til those goodie-goodies try the MEANER'S RED ANT JELLO." Nyuk, nyuk, nyuk.

The next morning the Meaner was fast out the door with his two huge sacks—one full of Meaner Beaner valentines, one full of Meaner Beaner snacks.

The kids in Ms. Barnyard's class could hardly wait for party time at the end of the day. The sacks of party food were heaped high on one table in the classroom, and valentines were heaped high on another. The Meaner's two sacks were sitting in the corner of the room, and whenever he looked at them his meaner eyes beamed with excitement.

Pavlov brought a huge information poster into the classroom—and it was all about Valentine 's Day. As every kid knew, Pavlov was the smartest dog in all of Tin City, and the smartest student in Ms. Barnyard's class. Though he could not talk, the genius dog carried with him a small slate board and some chalk, and that is how he got his messages to everyone – he chalked his talk. The kids learned many new and exciting things by reading Pavlov's poster. They learned that this special day may have been named after an ancient Roman, Saint Valentine, who died on February 14, in the year 269 A.D. The kids gathered round the poster, and they read all of the interesting facts and looked at all the pictures that Pavlov had downloaded from the internet. All the kids felt very lucky that Pavlov was in Ms. Barnyard's class.

By 2:30 it was almost party time. The kids all left for their last recess of the day, but the Meaner Beaner sneaked back to the empty classroom. First, he emptied the children's valentines into the huge garbage pail, and then he set out his own MEANER BEANER VALENTINES to the desks. Then, he emptied the children's party food into another huge garbage pail and set out the MEANER BEANER PARTY FOOD. When the bell rang the kids came in full of energy, ready for the party.

"First," said Ms. Barnyard, "we will open our valentines. William was the mailman and he has kindly delivered them to your desks."

Goose Anderson was excited. He really liked Julie Fonzio and he hoped that her valentine would be big and beautiful. Goose carefully opened the valentine. Inside was a poem from Julie.

**Dear Goose**
**On Valentine's Day**
**Will you be mine?**
**I hope NOT-NOT-NOT**
**Cause yer ugly face**
**Looks like FRANKENSTEIN!**
**From Julie**

Goose could not believe what he read. He shook his fist at her. "I hope you sit on a sharp tack!" he whispered to her. Julie was perplexed. She thought Goose would truly like her valentine. Why was he so upset?

Frannie O'Neill held her breath. She really liked Louie Gomez and she hoped his valentine would say wonderful things. Frannie carefully opened the valentine. Inside was a poem from Louie.

**Dear Frannie**
**When you are sitting in your chair,**
**I can only sit and stare**
**Cause your pants are full of MICE**
**And your hair...is full of LICE!**
**From Louie**

Frannie glared across the room at Gomez, sitting in his wheelchair. "I hope your cat gets fleas," she whispered to him. Louie was perplexed. He had written such a special poem. Why was Frannie so upset?

Sadie's Orson's heart was pounding. She hoped stuttering Billy Taberham would send her a special valentine, big and red and full of warm words. But as all the kids knew, Sadie was the 'worry wart' of the class. She worried about everything. Yesterday she worried that it was going to rain and she would get her new dress ruined. On Wednesday she worried that she was going to fail the spelling test and on Tuesday she worried that her cat would run away. Sadie worried as she opened the red valentine. Inside was a poem from Billy.

**Dear S...S...Sadie**
**When I look and see you th...th...there,**
**The s...s...sunlight shining on your hair,**
**I really know by n...n...now**
**You look like an old brown C...C...COW!**
**From B...B...Billy**

Sadie shook her fist at Billy and whispered, "I hope your underwear turns purple." Billy was perplexed. Why was Sadie so upset? He had worked for hours on her valentine.

After fifteen minutes of opening valentines, the classroom turned graveyard quiet. There were long, sad faces on all of the children. Now, Ms. Barnyard was perplexed. This was supposed to be a fun party. Didn't the kids like getting valentines? In the very back desk the Meaner Beaner tried very hard to put a sad look on his face, but he was laughing on the inside.

"Well," Ms. Barnyard finally said, "we should cheer up this classroom and have our special treats." The kids instantly forgot about the valentines and they all cheered. "Mouse Krause," said Ms. Barnyard, "let's start with those jam sandwiches you brought. They look so delicious!" Little Mouse proudly passed out the sandwiches.

When the kids bit into the sandwiches, they began coughing and hacking. Some of the kids ran out of the room, straight for the toilet. "AAAAAAAAAUGGHHHH, THESE SANDWICHES TASTE LIKE CAT FOOD," they all yelled out at once. Mouse had tears in her eyes, and at the back of the room the Meaner Beaner was chuckling, "Nyuk, nyuk, nyuk."

"Well, class," said Ms. Barnyard, "Perhaps those sandwiches were just sitting out too long and became spoiled. It's not Mouse's fault. Let's have some of Abby Willshire's fruit punch to wash them down."

Abby proudly poured her fruit punch into the paper cups. On the count of three they all took a big, fast gulp. The class began gasping and spraying the bad tasting punch out of their mouths. Some of the students fell out of their desks and onto the floor. "THIS PUNCH TASTES

LIKE VINEGAR!" they all yelled out at once. Abby had a big lump in her throat, and in the back seat the Meaner Beaner was filled with glee.

"Well," said Ms. Barnyard, "perhaps the punch was sitting in the sun too long and became sour. It's not Abby's fault. Let's have some nice treats to end the party. Marjorie Kell, please pass out your Jell-O dessert, and Naj Singh please pass out your Creamo cookies. They will be delicious!"

Naj proudly handed out the Creamo cookies, and Marjorie proudly scooped the Jell-O into bowls. The class quickly chomped down the cookies. But all at once they began sputtering and spitting the cookies out onto the desktops. "THESE COOKIES TASTE LIKE SHOE POLISH!" they all yelled out at once. To get rid of the bad tasting cookies they quickly spooned the red Jell-O into their mouths. In the next instant hundreds of little red ants were crawling out of mouths, across faces, into noses, and down, down into underpants. "YUCK! YUCK! YUCK!" they all screamed. Some of the kids rolled onto the floor and madly scratched their bums. At the back of the room the Meaner Beaner could hardly control his laughter.

Just then, Sadie Orson picked up a handful of Jell-O and threw it at Marjorie, but Marjorie ducked and the Jell-O hit Mouse Krause square in the face. Little Mouse threw a Creamo cookie at Naj but it veered off and hit Joe Ford in the nose. Joe Ford threw a sandwich at Billy Taberham, but the sandwich hit Frannie's ear. Frannie threw a cup of punch at Goose Anderson, but it missed and hit Ms. Barnyard.

The classroom was suddenly in a wild food fight. The walls became plastered with cat-food sandwiches, the desks were a mess of shoe-polish cookie crumbs, the

windows were smeared with red-ant Jell-O, and the floor was slimy with vinegar punch.

Suddenly, there was a loud knock on the classroom door, and Mr. Cramm, the principal, stormed into the room. "WHAT IS GOING ON HERE!" he bellowed out. But no one heard the principal and poor Mr. Cramm was pelted with Jell-O and sandwiches and cookies and vinegar punch, just like everyone else.

Finally, the day was done. The sun was setting as the Brickstreeters walked quietly home. It had taken them three hours to clean the classroom and Mr. Cramm had given them a one-week class detention. The Meaner Beaner ran up to the group. His chest was puffed and he had a mean sneer on his face. "So you goodie-goodies had your Valentines Day ruined," and he gave them all the Meaner chuckle: Nyuk, nyuk, nyuk. "I guess you pinheads didn't have such a good time today, did you?" Nyuk, nyuk, nyuk. The Meaner was laughing so hard he nearly fell into a slush puddle.

Just then little Mouse Krause stepped forward. "Meaner, what are you talking about? Weren't you at the party today? Those valentines were HILARIOUS! And the food fight was TERRIFIC! We don't know who did all those things, but THAT WAS THE BEST PARTY WE EVER HAD!"

"YAH, YAH," the kids all cheered. "THAT WAS THE BEST PARTY IN THE HISTORY OF BRICK STREET SCHOOL!"

The Meaner Beaner turned and walked away from them. He shook his head and kicked a stone. "Rats," he grumped, "I HATE IT WHEN THOSE GOODIE-GOODIES HAVE FUN!" And then he said to himself in a low voice, "Just wait, Brickstreeters. Just wait for next year's

Valentine's Day party. I will caper you real good. I will
caper you real good."

# Chapter Two

## Pet Day

The first week of muddy March was always Pet Day in Ms. Barnyard's class. "Remember, children, tomorrow is Pet Day," she told them. To be sure they would not forget, Ms. Barnyard had all of her students write it down in their Day Planners. She did not want any of the children to forget to bring in their favorite pet. "And remember too," she told them, "be prepared to introduce your pet to our class, and tell us a little bit about your little friend."

Sadie Orson, the worry wart, put up her hand. "Ms. Barnyard," she said. "I am a little worried about Pavlov. Whom will Pavlov bring on Pet Day?"

Sadie always worried too much, but this time she was right. Whom would Pavlov bring to school on Pet Day? Pavlov was the only dog-student at Brick Street School. For sure, he was the smartest student in Ms. Barnyard's class, but, still, he was a dog. Ms. Barnyard turned to Pavlov and asked him: "Pavlov, whom will you bring to school on Pet Day?" All of the kids looked at the dog-student.

Pavlov adjusted his glasses and picked up his slate board. On the slate he chalked his one-word answer: **Surprise**. And so it was left. Tomorrow Pavlov would bring a pet to school, but, until then, it would be a surprise.

The Brickstreeters were wild with chatter all the way home from school. Mouse Krause walked with Sadie Orson. "I am going to give Digger a bath tonight," said little Mouse Krause. Nobody wants a stinking wiener dog in school. I am going to put my best perfume on Digger, so he smells just like a spring flower.

13

"Good idea," Sadie told her friend. "I am going to put a red bow around Figgy's neck. She will be the best-looking gerbil in Brick Street School. I just hope she doesn't bite anybody's fingers. I am a little worried about that. Figgy loves to bite fingers."

Naj Singh and stuttering Billy Taberham walked along together, while Louie Gomez rolled beside them in his wheelchair. "Pet Day is my favorite day of school," Naj said. "I am bringing Toby, and tonight I am going to brush his hair 50 times. He will be the softest cat who has ever meowed at Brick Street School.

"Good for you," said Billy. "Tonight I am going to teach P...P...Pinky a new sentence. Then, every one will know it's true: I have the smartest m...m...mynah bird in Tin City.

"My favorite pet lives in a bowl in my bedroom," said Louie. He is an angel fish named Devil. Tomorrow he will see my classroom. Devil will be soooooooooooo happy!"

The Brickstreeters could talk of nothing else all the way home. Frannie O'Neill would bring her green frog, Lindy, with a little top hat on her head. Marjorie Kell would bring her brown monkey, Danny, dressed up in a blue suit, Joe Ford would bring his bull snake, Osborne, Goose Anderson would bring his pet pig, Oink, Annabelle Jefferson would bring Earl the Emu, and Pavlov would bring a surprise.

William Joseph Beaner walked behind the group. He could hear them talking and laughing, all excited about tomorrow. The Meaner Beaner HATED Pet Day at Brick Street School. He HATED WHEN OTHER KIDS HAD FUN. "Those goodie-goodies having fun on Pet Day," he told himself, sour as a piece of lemon. "That pains me more than a bee sting on my behind. I HATE PET DAY."

That night, the Meaner Beaner was unusually quiet. Up in his room, in his favorite Nightmare Pajamas, he grumped about Pet Day. "All those Brickstreeters will think they are so special, taking all their pets to school...They will all act so happy...They will be smiling and talking and laughing...I HATE IT WHEN THOSE BRICKSTREETERS HAVE FUN!"

Just then, the Meaner heard a sound from the corner of his bedroom: Chidder, chidder, chidder. He went over to the corner and looked at his best friend in the wire cage. With eyes like flaming red torches, Rat Zakary looked back at the Beaner. Zakary smiled an evil smile, his long razor-sharp teeth reflecting the desk light. "What are you smiling for, little friend?" the Meaner asked. "You would not like Pet Day. All of the animals must be very good at school, they must behave, they must mind their manners...all of the things you HATE, my little friend. You would not like Pet Day." But still, Rat Zakary continued to smile, and his eyes met the Meaner's eyes. Zakary focused on the Meaner, and Meaner focused on Zakary. They stared into each other's eyes for so long that their brains were locked together. And then, in that empty space between them, an idea surged like an electric current, from Zakary's brain, through the empty space, right into the Meaner's brain. He had been ZAPPED, and at that instant, the Meaner began to smile.

"Oh, Zakary, you are right. Maybe, we could have some great fun on Pet Day. We could have some very wicked fun, some truly evil fun. We could RUIN Pet Day at Brick Street School. Yes, we will DESTROY Pet Day at Brick Street School." Nyuk, nyuk, nyuk. That night, the Meaner had a good sleep. He could hardly wait until Pet Day!

The next day, Ms. Barnyard's classroom was like a zoo.

Every Brickstreeter had a pet. There were 3 birds, 2 dogs, 5 cats, a gerbil, a monkey, a pig, a green frog, a bull snake, and one furry rat with razor-sharp teeth. It was the BEST DAY—even William Joseph Beaner was happy!

All morning the kids fed and watered their pets. They brushed them and washed them and kept all cages clean. In art class they drew pictures of their pet; in math they completed bar graphs about their pet; in science they did pet experiments; they read pet stories during reading time and wrote pet stories during writing time. Then, at eleven o'clock, just after the lunch hour, the kids introduced their little and not-so-little friends.

Mouse Krause introduced her wiener dog, and she showed them how Digger could roll over, bark three times, and play dead. Sadie introduced Figgy, and the class watched as the gerbil ran on his spinning wheel at 100 miles per hour. Naj Singh introduced Toby, who had the softest, blackest fur in the whole town of Tin City. Stuttering Billy Taberham introduced P...P...P...Pinky, who had been trained to say his owner's name: B...B...B...Billy T...T...T...Taberham. Louie Gomez sat up proudly in his wheelchair and introduced his angel fish named Devil. Frannie O'Neill introduced the class to Lindy, her green frog with a top hat on his head. But, when Frannie commanded him to jump, Lindy just sat there, as motionless as a stone. "Jump, Lindy," she told him over and over, but Lindy just sat. Back in the corner one of the kids thought he heard the Meaner Beaner mumble to himself: "SSSSSTUPID FROG." Marjorie Kell's pet monkey, Danny, climbed all over Ms. Barnyard's desk and began eating the plasticine. Everyone laughed, except Ms. Barnyard. Joe Ford showed the class how he could pick up his bull snake, Osborne, and let it coil around his neck. The kids all gasped, thinking that Joe Ford would surely choke to death. But he didn't. The tallest pet in the room was Earl, Annabelle's pet emu, with its large eyes and eyelashes four inches long. Goose Anderson had his pet pig, Oink, on a leash, and Goose explained how smart pigs really were. Back in the corner one of the kids thought he heard the Meaner Beaner mumble to himself that the pig was probably smarter than Goose Anderson.

The kids noticed that Pavlov's desk was empty. They felt very bad. Perhaps he had no pet to take to school and so he stayed home. Perhaps he was embarrassed. Then, at ten minutes past one in the afternoon, there was a knock on the classroom door. When Ms. Barnyard opened the door, in walked Pavlov, and right behind him, walked a little boy. This was very strange.

"Who is this?" asked Ms. Barnyard. Pavlov answered on his slate board: **This is Jeremy, my pet boy. He is four years old. He likes chocolate candies. He cries when he is scared.**

The kids clapped their hands for Pavlov's pet, just as they had clapped for all the pets. Finally, it was the Meaner's turn to introduce his pet. But there was one more surprise...Rat Zakary was not in his cage! Ms. Barnyard was concerned: "William, where did Zakary go? Did he get out of his cage?"

The Meaner looked very sheepish. "Actually, Ms. Barnyard, he went home."

"Went home! What do you mean he went home? How could Zakary go home?"

"Oh, it's okay, Ms. Barnyard. Zakary is very smart. Smarter than Oink or Pinky or Toby or Digger or Jeremy. He knows how to find 11 Brick Street, go in the back window, and stay under the bed until I get home. He is

very smart. Smarter, even, than Goose Anderson."

"Well, William, I don't quite know what to think about this. I do hope that your pet is able to get home by himself...Well, class, we will just continue the day. Let's leave the pets for a while and do some quiet reading. Then, it will be time for cleanup."

The kids all read quietly. Suddenly, a knock came to the classroom door. The kids all looked up. The pets looked up. It was the kindergarten teacher from down the hall. She came into the classroom, holding the hand of a little kindergarten boy. The little boy was wailing, over and over, "WHAAAAAAAA, WHAAAAAAAAAA, WHAAAA," and he was frightening Jeremy and all the other pets.

"What is the matter?" asked Ms. Barnyard. "What is the matter with the little kindergarten boy?"

"Something TERRIBLE has happened!" announced the kindergarten teacher. "The WHOLE CLASS is crying and I can't get them to stop."

"The whole class is crying?" asked Ms. Barnyard. "What happened? Did they all sit on sharp tacks?"

"No, no, no," said the kindergarten teacher. "At one-thirty every day, the kindergartners have their afternoon snack. But someone has eaten today's snack. Every snack was eaten, and now there are only a few crumbs left. Does anybody in this class know who might have eaten the kindergarten snacks? Who would ever do such a wicked thing?"

The little boy continued to wail, "WHAAAAAAAAA, WHAAAAAAA, WHAAAA," but the kids sat silently. They had no idea.

Mouse Krause put up her hand and asked, "What kind of snack did the kindergartners have today?"

The kindergarten teacher said, "Cheese and crackers.

All of the cheese and crackers were eaten. Only crumbs were left." Someone in the class thought that they heard the Meaner chuckle, Nyuk, nyuk, nyuk, and mumble to himself, "I know someone who likes cheese and crackers very much." Nyuk, nyuk, nyuk.

The classroom had calmed down and the kids got back to their reading, but in fifteen minutes, another knock came to the door. In came a little grade-3 girl from across the hall. She was soaking wet and wailing loudly, "WHAAAAAAA, WHAAAAAAAA, WHAAAAAAAA." The kids all looked up in amazement and the pets stared at the little girl with eyes wide open.

Ms. Barnyard jumped up from her chair. "What is it little girl, what is the matter? Why are you all wet? Why are you crying?"

Through her sobs, the little girl managed to blurt out the story. "I left my class...I went to the washroom...I was sitting on the toilet...Then I heard something in the toilet...I peeked down into the toilet...and something was in there swimming, SOMETHING BROWN AND UGLY, WITH LONG SHARP TEETH AND RED EYES...WHAAAAAAA. WHAAAAAAA, WHAAAAAAA...I became so frightened, I FELL INTO THE TOILET!"

After that, someone thought they had heard the Meaner give his chuckle, Nyuk, nyuk, nyuk, and mumble to himself, "I know someone who likes to swim in the toilet." Nyuk, nyuk, nyuk.

The kids could hardly believe what they had heard. They felt so bad for the girl, but Ms. Barnyard managed to get the little grade-3 back to her classroom, and the kids once again settled into their reading. Then, just fifteen minutes before the end of school, a knock once again came to the classroom door. In stepped Mr. Cramm, the school principal. He wanted to chat with Ms. Barnyard about the class trip next week. But as they stared at the school principal, the kids could not believe their eyes. At first, some of the kids began snickering. Then, more snickering. Even Ms. Barnyard began snickering. The snickering became louder and louder, until everyone in the class was laughing. Roaring with laughter. Some of the kids were laughing so hard they fell out of their desks. Ms. Barnyard was laughing so hard, she fell to the floor, and began rolling around the carpet. Even the pets in their cages were staring at the principal. Digger began howling in laughter, Figgy squeaked, Toby meowed, Pinky squawked, Lindy croaked, Danny let out a monkey-squeal and jumped on top of Ms. Barnyard's head. Osborne hissed in laughter, the angel fish named Devil glubbed a bubble, Oink the Pig squealed and squealed, Earl the Emu blinked and blinked its long eyelashes and Pavlov's pet boy Jeremy giggled and giggled.

Finally, Mrs. Barnyard managed to say, "Mr. Cramm, go look in the mirror over there, go look in the mirror."

Mr. Cramm rushed over to the mirror and was instantly stunned at what he saw. The wig on the top of his head was a complete mess, all ruffled up and crooked and, rising from the back, where his cowlick should have been, was a huge rat's tail sticking straight up into the air. Somehow a rat had made a nest in his wig! "Oh, no, oh no," yelled Mr. Cramm, afraid to even touch the rat's nest on his head, and the kids and pets continued to howl, squeak, meow, squawk, croak, monkey-squeal, hiss, glub, pig-squeal, blink and giggle.

Suddenly, the rat popped out of the wig and ran all the way down Mr. Cramm onto the floor. "IT'S RAT ZAKARY!" all the kids yelled at once. And in a second, Rat Zakary ran up Frannie's arm. Frannie stopped laughing and started to yell. She was terrified of rats. The rat ran down Frannie, across the room and into Naj Singh's black hair. "Get out, get out," Naj yelled. He too was terrified of rats. The rat ran down Naj, across the floor, across little feet, across desks, across fingers, and the whole class began yelling and screaming. Everyone in the class was terrified of rats! Even the animals in the class began sounding out in fear: Digger barked ferociously, Figgy squeaked in horror, Toby gave a mad-cat screech, Pinky squawked in horror, thinking she was going to die, Lindy croaked, and for the first time began jumping and jumping, Danny gave loud, fearful monkey squeals, and jumped on Oink the Pig. Osborne, the bull snake, coiled up and hissed his warning to stay away, the angel fish named Devil glubbed a gigantic bubble, and Oink, with the monkey on his back, was pig-squealing so loudly he sounded like a fire truck. Earl the Emu blinked its long eyelashes faster than ever, and Pavlov's pet boy Jeremy giggled and giggled. Jeremy liked rats.

Sadie, the worry wart, started to whine: "I knew this was going to be awful. I just knew it." At the back of the class, the Meaner Beaner was chuckling madly, Nyuk, nyuk, nyuk, and someone heard him mumble to himself, "I LOVE PET DAY, IT'S THE BEST DAY OF THE YEAR." Nyuk, nyuk, nyuk.

Finally the day was done. Rat Zakary had scurried from the room and was not seen for the rest of the school day. The kids stayed in an extra hour, cleaning the classroom, Mr. Cramm gave them all a week's detention, and Ms. Barnyard announced that there would be no more Pet Days at Brick Street School. NO MORE PET DAYS EVER!

That night, the Meaner Beaner looked under his bed. In the darkness, far under the bed, he could see the fiery red eyes of his one true friend. He spoke to him: "Come here my little friend, come here, and I will put you back into your cage." The rat started moving towards the Meaner Beaner. "You liked Pet Day, didn't you, little friend. You liked Pet Day because you got to eat cheese and crackers and swim in the girl's toilet and make a nest in the principal's wig and scare kids and scare other pets. You got to do very bad things today, and it was fun, wasn't it my little friend?" Zakary came closer and closer to the Meaner.

The Meaner could see now that the rat was not smiling. Rat Zakary was not happy. He looked angry. The Meaner picked up Zakary and then he saw something...Rat Zakary had no tail! No tail! Zakary's tail had gone missing! Just then, the phone rang, Meaner quickly put Zakary into his cage and answered.

On the other end of the line was Joe Ford. Joe sounded a little out of breath, a little confused about something. "Meaner," he said.

"Yeah, what is it Ford? What do you want?"

"Meaner, I just called to see if your pet was okay. I just went over to check on Osborne."

"Yeah, so what"" the Meaner grumped. "So what? Bull snakes are SSSSSTUPID pets anyway."

"Well, said Joe, I went over to give Osborne some food and water and I noticed something sticking out the side of his mouth...Something very unusual...At first I thought it was a rope, but when I got closer, I could see that it was not a rope...I could see what it really was...It was a long, brown, furry RAT'S TAIL."

The Meaner hung up the phone on Joe Ford. He yelled

out in his room: "That SSSSTUPID Osborne! That SSSSTUPID Joe Ford! It's like I always said: I HATE PET DAY!"

# Chapter Three

## The Super Sleepover

Frannie O'Neill loved green. Every day she wore something green—a green sweater, maybe, or green jeans, or green socks, or a green ribbon in her hair. If she had no green on the outside, the kids all knew for sure—Frannie's underwear must surely be green. When Frannie went to Jimmi Ho's Chinese General Store for a giant ice cream cone, she would always choose pistachio. Her lunch box was always green with something—grapes, maybe, or a lime, or an unripe banana. Frannie chewed green gum and did all of her homework in green ink. Ms. Barnyard didn't care, as long as her homework was done.

March 17, St. Patrick's Day, was Frannie's favorite. It was her birthday. This year was very special, because Frannie would be ten years old. Finally. All of her life, she had wanted to be ten years old. To celebrate her tenth year on the planet Earth, Frannie was having a Super Sleepover Birthday Party. All of the Brickstreeters were invited.

In the dim light of his bedroom, the Meaner Beaner opened the green envelope, and he read the letter to Zakary:

Dear Meaner Beaner:
You are invited to my 10th Birthday Party. It will be a Super Sleepover. Please bring your pajamas. THIS WILL BE THE BEST BIRTHDAY PARTY IN THE HISTORY OF BRICK STREET. Sorry Meaner, but at this birthday party—NO RATS ALLOWED!
Your Friend, Frannie

No rats allowed! Zakary's ears burned with those words, and he began squealing and squealing. Sleepover parties could be great fun for a little rat! The Meaner walked over to the rat cage, and the two friends looked hard into each other's eyes. "I am very sorry, little friend," he said to Zakary, and then he kissed the rat on the whiskers. Just then, as Zakary's whiskers touched the Meaner's face, an idea sparked its way, through skin and bone and fur and freckles, from the animal's brain all the way to the human brain. ZAPPO. An idea that was very bad—and very beautiful.

The Meaner spoke softly to Zakary: "Thank you, little friend, thank you for sending to me that very fine idea. On March 17, I will RUIN Frannie O'Neill's Super Sleepover. I WILL CAPER THE BIRTHDAY PARTY. And then, every kid in Tin City will know it's true: THEY DON'T CALL ME THE MEANER BEANER FOR NOTHING." Nyuk, nyuk, nyuk, went the Meaner Beaner. Chidder, chidder, chidder, went Rat Zakary

On the eve of St. Patrick's Day, the kids, one by one, arrived at Frannie O'Neill's house. The night sky was filled with rain and thunder. As the kids came in from the wet night, each of them had a gift for Frannie. From Benny Lee, she got a green jackknife; from Marjorie Kell, green glow-in-the-dark pajamas; from Abby Willshire some lemon-lime chewing gum, from stuttering Billy Taberham, a b...b...box of delicious kiwis; from Annabelle Jefferson a can of all-green crayons, from Joe Ford, a ten dollar bill; from Naj Singh, 200 green pencils; from Mouse Krause, a beautiful spotted lizard; from Sadie Orson, a jar of olives; from Goose Anderson, a green water pistol; and from the genius dog, Pavlov, a wonderful new book: Anne of Green

Gables.

At ten o'clock the Meaner Beaner finally arrived, wet as a duck, with a zipped-up backpack on his back. He was carrying a huge bouquet of flowers for Frannie. The kids were in awe: the trickster of Brick Street had brought the best gift of all! Could the Meaner Beaner be changing? Could he be turning into a normal kid? Frannie's eyes lit up. "Oh, thank you, thank you, thank you," she said to the Meaner, and she leaned over to catch the sweet scent of the beautiful bouquet. But, as Frannie's nose touched the flowers, a green bug-like critter hopped onto her nose, scurried up her forehead and became tangled in her hair. "AAAAAAAAAAAAAHHHHHHHHHHH," Frannie yelled out. "I HATE INSECTS. I HATE INSECTS. I HATE INSECTS."

Joe Ford quickly helped Frannie get the critter from her hair. They all turned to Pavlov: "What is it Pavlov? What is it?" Pavlov adjusted his glasses and chalked on his slate board. Not an insect, he informed them. This was an 8-legged critter. An arachnid. He identified the arachnid as a green lynx spider. Not poisonous, he assured all of them.

The Meaner Beaner was smiling like a cat in a fish market. The kids just shook their heads. They knew it was true: the Meaner would never change. He would never be normal. Over in a corner, Sadie Orson shivered, and she whispered to herself, "I am very worried about this Super Sleepover. Very worried."

By eleven o'clock the kids had forgotten about the green lynx spider. It was a wild, terrific party. They ate popcorn, drank green pop, listened to bee-bop rock-and-roll music at full blast, did the crazy-chicken dance, had a pillow fight, and played the hoola-boola game. Then, at midnight, Frannie turned the lights down low and told them the story of The Old Leprechaun.

The kids and dog listened quietly. It was a scary, thunderous night. Rain hit the windows like tiny steel pellets, and lightning flashed and flashed like the blinking of angry, yellow eyes. Frannie delivered her story in a low, slow voice. "The Old Leprechaun lives in the good dreams of all Irish people," she told them. "He uses spells of magic to help Irish people and to protect them against the dangers of the world—especially the Night Scratcher." The sky thundered once again.

"Who is the N...N...Night Scratcher?" asked stuttering Billy Taberham.

The room was stone quiet as Frannie explained. "The Night Scratcher lives in our bad dreams and tries to come out and frighten us. He has red eyes and a long hook on one hand. He likes to scratch little kids like us." Sadie Orson looked very, very worried, but Frannie reminded them all: "The Old Leprechaun protects all Irish people from the Night Scratcher. We don't have to worry about the Night Scratcher because the Old Leprechaun will protect us. He will protect us tonight."

Sadie spoke up: "But we are not Irish, Frannie! Julie Fonzio is only Italian and Joe Ford is only English and Louie Gomez is only Mexican and Naj Singh is only East Indian and Mouse Krause is only German and Abby Willshire is only African American and I am only a little bit French and a little bit Welsh. None of us is Irish, Frannie, and I am very worried. Very worried."

"Don't be worried," Frannie told them all. The Old Leprechaun protects Irish people and their friends. You are my friends. The Old Leprechaun will protect all of you."

It was then that the Meaner piped up: "The Old

Leprechaun is SSSSSTUPID!"

The kids were stunned. They were shocked at what the Meaner had said. "It is not a good idea to say that a leprechaun is stupid," Frannie said. "I am Irish, and I know about things like that." The kids all shook their heads, completely agreeing with Frannie O'Neill. Even Pavlov, smartest in the room and a Russian Beagle himself, shook his head and agreed with Frannie.

The Meaner gave them his famous chuckle, the one they had heard a million times before: Nyuk, nyuk, nyuk. Nyuk, nyuk, nyuk. The night sky thundered and a flash of angry lightning lit up the room.

At two hours past midnight, Frannie turned on the night light, all of the kids got into their pajamas, and they jumped under the covers of the giant water bed. They were sooooooo tired. One by one, each of the kids drifted off to sleep. Every kid wanted to have a good dream.

Suddenly, in the thunderous night, there came another sound. Not the rain, but something different, something strange. It was a scratching sound. Mouse Krause heard it first, and she whispered to the others: "Wake up, wake up. Something is scratching on the bedroom window. The kids opened their eyes and looked outside. And there, staring back at them from the dark, wet night, were two blood-red eyes. The kids all screamed: AAAAAAAAAAHHHHHHH, and Mouse Krause yelled, "What is it, Pavlov? What is it?"

The kids quickly looked at Pavlov's slate board. He had written only two words: **Bad Dream**. "Oh no," wailed Sadie Orson. It is the Night Scratcher! He has escaped from someone's bad dream! He has come to scratch us! He has come to scratch us!" The kids pulled the enormous blanket over them, and they shivered and shivered in their dark world. Once again the night sky thundered and the kids and dog heard one small chuckle: Nyuk, nyuk, nyuk. Nyuk, nyuk, nyuk. It took a long time, but at last they were all asleep once again.

It was Joe Ford who next heard the sound in the night. The scratching, scratching, scratching outside the bedroom door. Joe screamed out in the night, AAAAAHHHGGGGG, and all of them sat up in bed. They all asked at once: "Pavlov, what is it? What is it?" Once again, Pavlov chalked out his answer, **Bad Dream**. Sadie Orson wailed and wailed: "It's the Night Scratcher! He is getting closer! I don't want to be scratched! I don't want to be scratched! I want to go home." Under one corner of the blanket there once again came the chuckle: Nyuk, nyuk, nyuk. Nyuk, nyuk, nyuk.

At three hours past midnight, Marjorie Kell sat up in bed. "Help, help," she cried out. Help me. I can't swim."

The kids awoke. Mouse Krause tried to be a friend: "It's okay, Marjorie. You were having a bad dream. You thought you were in the river. You thought you could not swim. I will turn on the light for you." But when Mouse turned on the light, they were all terrified at what they saw. It was true: THEY WERE SLEEPING IN WATER! And slowly, slowly the water was rising in the bedroom. Soon, their pillows were wet, their enormous blanket was wet, and their pajamas were all wet. The water rose higher and higher. Tooth brushes and slippers and hair brushes were now floating in the room. The night light was completely under water.

Just then, Marjorie Kell yelled out: "AAAAAAHHHHH, something is biting my big toe!" She reached down and pulled up from the water a spotted water snake. Joe Ford screamed out, reached down, and pulled up from the water an electric eel. The water was filled with strange, strange creatures—oysters, minnows, tadpoles, water spiders, mud turtles and a baby octopus. The kids yelled and screamed and swam to the bedroom door. Benny Lee and Joe Ford pulled hard on the door, and when it opened, the water poured out and, finally, the bedroom was a river no more.

Pavlov knew what had happened. All of the kids knew what had happened. In the dark, dark night, the Night Scratcher had come into the bedroom and scratched a hole in Frannie's giant water bed. Sadie Orson whined and whined. "I KNEW THIS WAS GOING TO BE A TERRIBLE SUPER SLEEPOVER. I JUST KNEW IT!" Over in the corner the Meaner Beaner chuckled his Meaner chuckle: Nyuk, nyuk, nyuk. Nyuk, nyuk, nyuk.

It took the kids and Pavlov two hours to dry out. They all helped to dry the floor with towels. It was now late, late, late, and the kids were falling-down tired. The waterbed was gone, so they slept under a blanket on the floor. In seconds, everyone was fast asleep, trying hard to dream the good dream. Outside the bedroom window, the sky made a thunderous growl and once again flashed its angry eyes. It was Billy Taberham who heard the next sound. Scratch, scratch, scratch. He got out of bed, tiptoed to the bedroom door, bent down and looked through the keyhole. AAAAAAAAUUUUUUUGGGGGGG, he screamed, and every human and dog sat bolt upright on their floor-bed. And he told them all: "I S...S...SAW IT, I S...S...SAW IT. OUTSIDE THE D...D...DOOR. IT HAD B...B...BLOOD-RED EYES. IT HAD T...T...TEETH TWENTY INCHES LONG AND CLAWS AS LONG AS CARPENTER N...N...NAILS."

The dog and kids all hugged each other, and the Meaner Beaner chuckled in the night: Nyuk, nyuk, nyuk. Nyuk, nyuk, nyuk.

It was Benny Lee who first noticed the problem. "Oh no," he said to them, "the rear end is gone from my pajamas! I HAVE NOTHING BUT BARE BUM!"

When he said that, all of the kids checked their own rear ends. Gone. All gone. Every rear end was missing from every pajama bottom. Bare bums were sticking out everywhere. Even Pavlov's pajamas had the rear end missing, and now his tail was sticking out. Sadie Orson wailed and wailed: "THIS IS TERRIBLE, HORRIBLE. THE NIGHT SCRATCHER HAS SCRATCHED THE REAR ENDS FROM OUR PAJAMAS! I AM WORRIED ABOUT THIS. VERY WORRIED."

Under the great cover, where no one could hear, the Meaner chuckled to himself: Nyuk, nyuk, nyuk. "This is the best Super Sleepover in the history of Brick Street."

It was very, very late in the night when the kids got to sleep for the last time. They could hear the rain on the windows: rattle, rattle, rattle. They all slept on their backs because their bare bums were cold. They stayed close to each other, hoping mightily that no one would again have a bad dream.

Then, it was early in the morning. The rain and thunder were gone, and the warm morning sun came streaming into the bedroom. The kids and dog heard one more sound. Not a scratch this time, but something different. They all heard it. It was a knock on the bedroom door. A very soft, gentle knock. All of them stood on the floor as Billy Taberham got up and looked through the key hole. "What is it, Billy? What is it?" the kids asked.

Billy turned and smiled. "L...L...Look what I have f...f...found," he told them, and he opened the door. The kids could not believe their eyes! Sitting in the doorway, in a tiny chair, all tied up, was the Night Scratcher. But this Night Scratcher had not come from someone's bad dream, no. The kids all knew that this little scratcher had come from a cage in one corner of William Joseph Beaner's bedroom. The Night Scratcher was Rat Zakary.

Zakary's arm claws were tied behind the chair. His leg claws were tied to the chair. He had a cloth tied around his mouth so he could not chidder. And Rat Zakary did not look the same. He had changed. Zakary's fur was no longer chocolate brown. Rat Zakary had become green, green, green. He was as green as a grasshopper. The Meaner was not chuckling now. He was gritting his teeth. He was boiling hot with anger.

All of the kids stood in their bare-bum pajamas. They stared at the green rat. Finally, Billy Taberham asked the question to the smartest one in the room: "P...P...Pavlov. "Wh...Wh...What happened? Who did this to R...R...Rat Z...Z...Zakary?" All of the kids waited as Pavlov chalked the slate board—and then he showed them his two-word answer. He wrote it in capital letters: OLD LEPRECHAUN.

The kids laughed and laughed and laughed. The Old Leprechaun had protected them all—because every one of them was a friend of the Irish girl. At this moment Pavlov and the kids knew it for sure: this had been the BEST SUPER SLEEPOVER IN THE HISTORY OF BRICK STREET. Pavlov and the kids—all except for one—turned to Rat Zakary and they said, all of them together, NYUK, NYUK, NYUK, NYUK, NYUK, NYUK, NYUK, NYUK.

# Chapter Four

## The Meaner Takes the Test of the Three Skulls

It was a windy Friday night and William Joseph Beaner could hear the window panes rattle, rattle, rattle. He made his way over to Zakary's cage. His little friend looked very good. A truly handsome rat – his tail had grown back, longer and better looking than ever. The Meaner rolled up his pajama sleeve, for he wanted to show his best friend the stone-hard muscle of his arm. "I am ready for THE TEST, Zakary. I am ready for the test. Tomorrow is the day. I am ready for my test." The Meaner flexed his arm muscle. "I have been doing fifty pushups every night. I am as strong as a cow. I have been practicing my mean looks in the mirror every night. I can look as mean as the junkyard dog. I have been playing dirty rotten tricks on all the Brickstreeters. I am as wily as a snake, Zakary, as wily as a snake." Zakary shivered when he heard the word 'snake.' Rat Zakary hated snakes.

When the Meaner went to bed, he was as excited as a Mexican jumping bean. Tomorrow he would take the test. And he was ready.

On Saturday morning, the Meaner walked east on Brick Street, past Brick Street Park, and cut south on Huckleberry. He made his way east again on Hog Street, all the way to the end, north on Dickerson Avenue, over the bridge at McGreggor's Creek, past the Junkyard, past Jimmi Ho's Chinese General Store, through the Mosquito Woodlot, across the train tracks, and on to Oak Street.

Oak Street was a dirty street. The alley cats were dirty, the dogs were dirty, and the kids were dirty. Oak Street was also a tough street. It was home to the dreaded Freddy

Sledgehammer Gang—the dirtiest, toughest gang in town. And, toughest of all, was Freddy Sledgehammer himself, the cold-hearted teenager with a skull and crossbones tattooed on his bald head. Freddy liked to scare kids with his rock-hard fist—he called it "THE SCREAMING SLEDGEHAMMER."

As the Meaner walked further south on Oak Street, the sky slowly darkened, and the wind hissed through the trees like a mad cat. The wooden fences were high and covered with bad words, some words the Meaner Beaner did not even know. The Meaner looked through the knot holes of the fence. He thought he could see eyes looking at him, and his knees started to shake a little. Maybe he should run back home, but no, he kept walking, walking, walking. He made his way further south and crossed the railroad tracks. This was the darkest, coldest, dirtiest, toughest place in the whole world. The Meaner thought that this would be a good place to live.

Finally, the Meaner was at the very end of Oak Street. He spotted the dark alley. Slowly, slowly, he walked up to the alley and looked down. He could see two far-away eyes peering out from the darkness. With hands in his pockets, the Meaner walked into the alley, all the way up to the eyes. The Meaner was sweating like a pig in the hot sun.

From the other side of the fence came a gruff, whispery voice: "What are you doing here, kid? What do you want?"

"I want to do THE TEST," said the Meaner Beaner. "I want to do THE TEST."

"Come with me," said the voice. "We will go and see Freddy." The Meaner followed the figure. In the dark alley he could faintly see that the boy was very tall and very wide. The Meaner looked at the boy's head—it was shaved bald, with a sledgehammer tattooed over his right ear. The

Meaner liked his bald head.

He was led, finally, to the clubhouse room. There were old crates for chairs, a cracked barrel for a table, and pictures of skeletons painted on the walls. The Meaner Beaner liked this room. Several boys were in the room—all were bald and all had sledgehammers tattooed over their right ears.

Then, the leader of the Sledgehammers entered the room. Freddy Sledgehammer was the meanest of all, the toughest of all, and his own bald head showed the leader's tattoo: the skull and crossbones. "Sit down, Beanbag," said Freddy. "Now what do you want?" Freddy's voice was like a can of gravel.

"Well, Freddy," the Meaner said meekly, "I would like to join the Sledgehammers." When the Meaner said that, all of the Sledgehammers in the clubhouse chortled. Even the mighty  Freddy chortled. "You are a Brickstreeter. A Brickstreeter can NEVER be a Sledgehammer! NEVER!"

The Sledgehammers shook their heads in complete agreement. "Never, never," they mumbled.

The Meaner looked at the mighty Freddy sitting in his chair. "Why not, Freddy? Why can't I become a Sledgehammer?"

Freddy glared at the Meaner Beaner. "Because," he said, "you cannot pass the TEST OF THE THREE SKULLS. A Brickstreeter could NEVER pass the TEST OF THE THREE SKULLS!"

The Meaner looked at Freddy, he looked at all the Sledgehammers standing around the clubhouse, and then he said firmly: "Yes I CAN Freddy! I CAN pass the TEST OF THE THREE SKULLS! I WANT to take the test!"

Freddy stared into the Meaner's green eyes. There was a long silence. "Very well," he said in his leathery voice.

"We will give you the test. Listen very carefully." Freddy told Meaner every detail:

> "You will be given three envelopes. Inside each envelope is a paper skull. On each skull is written a test. You must do one of the skulls each day for three days. You may fail one skull. You may fail two skulls. But you may NOT fail three skulls. If you fail all three skulls, you will fail the test and you will NEVER become a Sledgehammer. You will always be a BEANBAG. But if you pass JUST ONE skull, then you will pass the test and you will become a SLEDGEHAMMER."

Freddy handed to Meaner the three envelopes. "Remember: you have three days to do the test. When you are finished, you must come back to Oak Street and we will meet. Good luck, Beanbag." The Meaner took the three envelopes and walked back to Brick Street.

That night, in his room, the Meaner Beaner opened the first envelope. He read it to Rat Zakary:

---

**Skull Number One - you will not fail**
**If you snip and save a little girl's pigtail!**

---

The Meaner began to laugh. Nyuk, nyuk, nyuk. "This will be easy, Zakary. Mouse Krause has two very nice pigtails. When tomorrow is done, she will have only one!" Nyuk, nyuk, nyuk. Chidder, chidder, chidder, went Rat Zakary.

The next day was windless, sunny and bright, and late in the afternoon the Meaner made his way to 24 Brick, Mouse Krause's house. He knew that she played in her backyard every day after school. Slowly, slowly, he walked up to the fence around Mouse's backyard. He could hear the girls playing. They were giggling and having a good time. The Meaner listened, as quiet as a fox outside a chicken coop. Just then, he saw it—a pigtail was sticking through a crack in the fence. Mouse Krause's beautiful brown pigtail. Just what he needed.

The Meaner could hardly keep from laughing as he reached into his pocket and grabbed his pair of sharp scissors. With his other hand he quickly grabbed the pigtail—and snip. All at once, a loud roar came from the other side of the fence, and in a split second Mouse Krause's wiener dog, Digger, was racing around the corner, yelping ferociously. Digger had no tail. It had been snipped clean off! The Meaner ran for home, but the wiener dog caught up to him at the corner, biting his shoes, biting his socks, and biting the right leg off of his pants.

When the Meaner walked in the front door, he looked like a hobo: his shoes were ratty, his socks were shredded, he had one pant leg on and one pant leg off. He stormed up to his room. "Rats, rats, rats," he said to Zakary. "That SSSSSTUPID wiener dog made me fail my first skull. I HATE wiener dogs."

Later that night, the Meaner opened the second envelope and read it to Zakary:

> **For skull Number Two - we want to say,**
> **Bring us some cigarettes - but do not pay!**

The Meaner laughed: nyuk, nyuk, nyuk. "All I have to do is to steal some cigarettes." Nyuk, nyuk, nyuk. Chidder, chidder, chidder, went Rat Zakary

The next day the Meaner limped to school, and he limped back home. The dog bite was still hurting his foot.

But he did not care—for tonight he would pass Skull Number Two. He would no longer be a Beanbag. He would become a Sledgehammer.

Later that night the Meaner Beaner limped over to Jack's Pool Playing Hall on Donner Boulevard. He peered into the window. He could see some teenage girls in there. These were the girls who spent most of their time playing pool, smoking cigarettes, and spray-painting bad words on the alley walls. The Meaner kind of liked these girls. But, too bad, tonight he had a job to do. He had to cop a pack of cigarettes from them.

Slow as the midnight moon, the Meaner sneaked into the Pool Playing Hall. The juke box music was on, the girls were playing pool, Jack the owner was reading his paper, and no one paid much attention to the Meaner Beaner. One of the girls smiled at the Meaner, but they kept on playing pool. He spotted one girl's jean jacket on a bench, and he noticed the blue pack of cigarettes in the top pocket. Like a snake in the grass, the Meaner slithered over, copped the cigarettes and made his way out of the pool hall door. The Meaner limped quickly along the sidewalk towards home. Nyuk, nyuk, nyuk, he chuckled to himself. "I copped those cigarettes, I must say, and not one penny did I pay."

Half way home, the Meaner sat down on a park bench. He looked left, he looked right. No one around. The night was as quiet as a tomb. The Meaner reached into his pocket and pulled out the pack of cigarettes. "I want to be like the Sledgehammers," he said to himself. He took one out, put it in his mouth and lit it up. He took a long, hard puff. But the cigarette smoke was too much for the Meaner and he began hacking and coughing and choking. He grabbed his chest and fell to the ground. He hacked and coughed some more.

Just then, he heard voices on the sidewalk. "There's that kid," said one of the girls. "He stole my cigarettes!" The girls all ran towards the Meaner. He tried to get up and run, but the dog bite made him slow and in no time at all the girls had him in hand. Two girls held his hands behind his back and one girl reached into her purse. She brought out a spray can and began spraying the Meaner Beaner.

When the Meaner finally made it home, he turned on his bedroom light and looked into the mirror. His hair was now bright, bright orange. He looked so funny that even his best friend had to laugh: Chidder, chidder, chidder. "Rats, rats, rats," he said to Zakary. "I did not snip and save a pigtail, I did not cop a pack of cigarettes, but I still have Skull Number Three. I will pass this test. I will become a Sledgehammer. I will not be a Beanbag." The Meaner opened the third envelope. He read the third and last skull.

---

**You can be a Sledgehammer - if you're not a fool.
All you gotta do - is stink-bomb your school.**

---

"Stink-bomb the school!" the Meaner said, laughing and laughing. This is such a good caper. I will stink-bomb my school real good!" The Meaner laughed so hard he fell onto the floor and rolled under the bed. Rat Zakary laughed in his cage: Chidder, chidder, chidder.

That night, the Meaner went to the basement and opened his **Secret Box of No-Good Dirty Rotten Tricks** and took out five stink bombs and a gas mask. "This should do the job," he said to himself. Nyuk, nyuk, nyuk.

It was noon recess as the Meaner Beaner walked the playground of Brick Street School. He smiled to himself as he thought about his nefarious plan. He could see it all: When the bell rang, the kids would go into the school. He would put up his hand to go to the bathroom. In the bathroom, he would set off five stink bombs and put on his gas mask. In a few seconds, the whole school would be filled with a rotten, stinking smell. The kids would hold their noses and fall on the floor. The smell would be so bad, Mr. Cramm would have to clear the school. This would be the best, dirtiest trick he had ever played. And, best of all, he would no longer be a Beanbag. He would have a sledgehammer tattooed to his shaved head. He would be a member of Freddy Sledgehammer's gang. "Life is going to be sooooooooooo good," the Meaner told himself.

It was five minutes before the bell when the Meaner noticed a kindergarten kid riding his tricycle. He decided to tease the little boy. "Hey, little kid! You ride that tricycle like an old goat. You don't know how to ride a tricycle."   Nyuk, nyuk, nyuk. The little boy looked up at the bully. He gave the bully a sneer. The Meaner sneered back at the little boy, and then looked away from him. It was almost time for the bell to ring.

It was a moment in time that would change everything. As the Meaner looked at his watch, the tricycle gathered speed, aimed directly at the teasing bully. The Meaner never saw him coming. SPPLLAAAAAAAAAAMMMO— the Meaner flew into the air, landed hard on the ground, and five stink bombs went off in his pocket. An enormous plume of blue smoke rose high into the air. The kids on the playground had to plug their noses. The smell was horrible. The Meaner Beaner smelled so bad that he was not allowed into school when the bell rang, and Ms.

Barnyard had to send him home for the rest of the day.

At home he took five baths with soap and water, but still the smell was horrible. His mother and father made him eat supper in the basement. Even Rat Zakary held his nose when the Meaner went into his bedroom. The Meaner smelled worse than a cow's back end, worse than a barnyard pig, worse than ten-day-old socks.

Poor Meaner Beaner. He had failed the Test of the Three Skulls. That night he sneaked out of his house and made his way to Oak Street. He limped along on his dog-bitten foot, with his hair as orange as a Halloween pumpkin, and smelling like a dead chicken. When people saw him coming, they would cross the street to the other side. He finally made it to the secret alley, and to the clubhouse door. The door squeaked open, but there were no bald-headed kids around. Freddy was not around. The place was as quiet as the moon. The Meaner sat on an old crate and closed his eyes. He was soooooooooo tired.

It was three hours later when the Meaner woke up from the sound of a squeaking door. But he could see no one. He could hear no one. He knew he had to get back home. When the Meaner got back home, he limped up to his room. Rat Zakary immediately pinched his nose. The Meaner flicked on the light and looked into the mirror. AAAAAAAAAAAAAUUUUUUUUGGGGGH, he yelled out. He could not believe what he saw! His pumpkin-orange hair was gone. His head had been shaved as bald as a chicken egg. The Meaner looked closer. Just over his right ear was...a tattoo. A small, blue tattoo. Not a sledgehammer. Not a skull and crossbones. No. It was the perfect tattoo of...a BEANBAG.

Over in his cage, Rat Zakary laughed and laughed. Chidder, chidder, chidder. Chidder, chidder, chidder.

# Chapter Five

## The Meaner Beaner Skips School

Summer vacation was right around the corner, and the kids at Brick Street School were counting the days. Sitting in their desks, working quietly on their math problems, the Brickstreeters day-dreamed of summer. For Joe Ford it was swimming in McGreggor's Creek, and for Abby Willshire it was fishing for carp. For Naj Singh it was playing basketball on the street, and for Julie Fonzio it was skipping rope in the park. In her day-dream of summer, Annabelle Jefferson was visiting her grandparents down on the farm, feeding the goats and chickens and ducks. In his day-dream, Goose Anderson was sitting outside Jimmi Ho's Chinese General Store, eating a giant butterscotch ice cream cone. Louie Gomez dreamed of racing his wheelchair through the warm mud of summer, and stuttering Billy Taberham dreamed of riding his d...d...dirt bike every d...d...day. The only one to worry about summer was Sadie Orson. "I hope we don't have a hurricane in August," she told herself. "I am very worried about hurricanes. Very worried." Pavlov day-dreamed of digging up old bones and reading lots of stories about Snoopy and Lassie and Rin Tin Tin. Summer was coming to the day-dreams of everyone. Only seven school days left.

Ms. Barnyard was ready to dismiss the class. "Tomorrow is Friday, and I will have a surprise for you. It is very important that everyone comes to school tomorrow," the teacher told her class. "Remember, there is still one week of school left, and this is no time to slack off. Come to school. Be prepared. Buckle down. Work hard."

When the bell rang the kids all rushed over to Brick Street Park. There was still an hour before dinner, time to have fun. Marjorie Kell and little Mouse Krause caught crayfish in McGreggor's Creek. Billy Taberham, Naj Singh and Benny Lee played marbles on the ball diamond. Sadie Orson and her friends made necklaces and bracelets from the stems of dandelions, and Pavlov sat on the park bench, reading a good book. It was a glorious day.

Finally it was time to go home for supper. But there was trouble. When Sadie came to get her bike, there was a huge gob of axle grease on the seat. When Billy came for his jacket, a green b...b...bullfrog was poking out of the pocket. When Marjorie Kell came to pick up her speller, it was covered with stink bugs. And when Pavlov went to get his slate board, it was painted red. Pavlov and the kids all looked around. They could not see the dirty trickster of Brick Street, but they knew he must be hiding somewhere.

It was no secret: William Joseph Beaner was the wiliest kid on the planet. He was a rascal, a scamp, a scalawag. The kids all knew that in his dark basement the trickster had his **Secret Box of No-Good Dirty Rotten Tricks**. No kid had ever seen that box, but they knew there were many sharp-gooey-slimy-stinky-prickly-crawly-yucky things inside. Where did the Meaner get the ideas for his rotten capers? No one knew for sure. "Rat Zakary is ZAPPING Meaner's b...b...brain with evil ideas," said Stuttering Billy Taberham. Still, they all wondered: Why was William so mean? No one knew, not even Pavlov, smartest in the class. But Frannie O'Neill whispered to them in the park one day that Meaner was not born the way they were all born. He was not born at the Tin City Hospital. He did not come from his mother. He was hatched from a rotten egg.

After supper some of the Brickstreeters went back to the park to play. On the way to the park Sadie, Billy and Marjorie met up with the Meaner Beaner.

Sadie put the question to the Meaner in her sharp, squeaky voice: "Hey, Meaner, did you grease my bike seat today at the park?"

"And did you b...b...bullfrog my j...j...jacket?" stuttered Billy.

"And did you stinkbug my speller?" Marjorie asked, pointing a finger at him.

Pavlov chalked a note: **And did you paint my slate board red?**

The Meaner's mouth slithered upwards into a reptile smile. "Why would I want to do bad things to you goodie-goodies?" and he finished off with the famous Meaner chuckle, Nyuk, nyuk, nyuk. The Meaner's voice then became low and gravelly. "I bet you goodies will stay up all night and study for Ms. Barnyard's pop test tomorrow.

"What pop test?" Marjorie replied. "Ms. Barnyard never said we were having a pop test tomorrow."

"She said she had a SURPRISE for us," said the Meaner. "And she told us to MAKE SURE we came to school tomorrow. She told us to BUCKLE DOWN. That means only one thing—it is going to be one of Ms. Barnyard's TERRIBLE, HORRIBLE POP TESTS! Arithmetic ...spelling... reading comprehension... I HATE POP TESTS!"

"If we have a p...p...pop test, it will p...p...probably be easy," said Billy. "There are only s...s...seven days left until s...s...summer holidays. Ms. Barnyard wouldn't give us a hard p...p...pop test."

"Don't be too sure, Taberham," said the Meaner, turning to walk home. "By the way, you pinheads should watch where you sit down...you never know where the red ants are crawling," and he gave them a final Meaner chuckle: Nyuk, nyuk, nyuk, nyuk.

When the Meaner walked in the front door, he could smell the delicious chicken stew his mom was making in the kitchen. His dad was in the living room, reading the Tin City newspaper. "Hello, William," he said to his son. "How was school today?"

"Hi, Daddy," said the Meaner, his voice as sugary as pancake syrup. "School was very good, and tomorrow Ms. Barnyard is going to give us a pop test. I love pop tests, Daddy."

The Meaner's mother came into the room. "You are such a smart boy, William. If you wash up, supper will be ready in fifteen minutes. We are having chicken stew."

When William finished the last spoonful of stew, he went to his room and talked to his finest friend, Rat Zakary. Zakary's red eyes glowed from the cage in the darkest corner of the room. "We are having a SSSSSTUPID pop test tomorrow, Zakary...I HATE pop tests." Zakary's lips curled into a wicked grin, his red eyes stared hard into the Meaner's green eyes and instantly a blue flash lit up the room. "Oh, Zakary, Zakary, Zakary, you have sent a wonderful caper into my meaner brain. Thank you, thank you." Nyuk, nyuk, nyuk, went the Meaner Beaner. Chidder, chidder, chidder, went Rat Zakary.

The Meaner switched on his desk light and wrote a note in his mother's best printing:

Dear Ms. Barnyard,
William is very sick and cannot come to skool today. Pleze do
not give him a Pop Test when he comes back, becuz that wud
not be fair.
Yours truly, Missus Beaner

The next morning the Meaner hurried out the door,
with Rat Zakary riding on his shoulder. It was a sparkling
June day as the Brickstreeters made their way to school.
The Meaner ran to catch up with Joe Ford. "Hey, Joe, stop
a minute," said the Meaner. "I have a note for you to give
to Ms. Barnyard." The Meaner tried to look sickly and he
pretended to cough. "I don't feel well today, and I won't be
going to school" He coughed again.

"Okay, Meaner," said Joe. "I will give it to Ms.
Barnyard...but it is very strange that you suddenly got a
bad cold on a warm June day...Are you sure you are not
playing one of your dirty, no-good Meaner Beaner tricks?"

"No, no, no," said the Meaner. "Now just give this to
Ms. Barnyard." The Meaner turned to go back home, but
he quickly sneaked behind a tree. Finally, he heard the
school bell ring. Nyuk, nyuk, nyuk, he chuckled. "It is a
good day to skip school—especially when those goodie-
goodies have to write a pop test." Nyuk, nyuk, nyuk.
Chidder, chidder, chidder, went Rat Zakary.

With Zakary on his shoulder the Meaner wandered
over to his favorite place—the Junkyard for No-good Cars.
There was a sign on the high wire fence.

**BEWARE OF JAKE,**
**THE JUNKYARD DOG**
**He likes to bite.**

The Meaner looked left. He looked right. No dog around. No one in sight. He quickly scaled the fence and dropped down inside the junkyard.

He ran over to a rusty old car, got inside and locked the doors. In his own mind the Meaner Beaner became a famous race car driver, and Zakary was his racing partner. He steered the steering wheel, braked the brake, and shifted the gears as he roared past other race cars, cut sharp corners and tramped hard on the gas peddle towards the checkered flag. "VVAAAAARRROOOOOM," he made the mighty engine go. The Meaner Beaner and Zakary had won the race!

Just then, the Meaner heard a sound outside the car. A low, unfriendly growl. "OH NO!" The Meaner and Zakary looked up. Just outside the driver's window stood Jake, the junkyard dog. The one who liked to bite. The Meaner Beaner began to sweat, and Zakary jumped onto his shoulder. Slowly, slowly, the Meaner moved across the seat and opened the passenger door, and then, like a cat in a thunderstorm, the Meaner dashed out of the car and made a run for the fence. Jake tore after the Meaner and Zakary, barking and howling. The Meaner ran faster, and Jake ran faster. Zakary was sure he would be eaten for dessert. When the Meaner reached the high wire fence, he climbed madly, but Jake jumped up and bit the Meaner's rear end.

YYYOOOOOOOOOOOOOOOOOOOWWWWW," the Meaner yelped, but he kept climbing. Zakary squealed and squealed. The Meaner reached the top and dropped down to the safe side of the fence. Reaching around, he felt the big hole in his favorite jeans. Only his polka dot underwear was showing. "Rats," grumbled the Meaner Beaner, and he thought about the day: "Well, the junkyard dog bit my rear end—BUT AT LEAST I DON'T HAVE TO WRITE THAT

SSSSSSSSSSSTUPID POP TEST." Nyuk, nyuk, nyuk. Chidder, chidder, chidder, went Zakary.

The Meaner and Zakary loved crayfishing, so they made their way to McGreggor's Creek, and sat on the grassy bank. The Meaner grabbed twenty crayfish from the icy water, and Zakary was able to claw two. The Meaner then decided to go to Grassy Park across the creek, but the walking bridge was far down. "I can jump this creek," the Meaner said to Zakary. "Hold on to my shoulder." He backed up and took a long run, but just before his take-off, the Meaner's foot hit a stone. The Meaner skidded, somersaulted in mid air, and the boy and rat splashed down in the icy water of McGreggor's Creek."

Poor Meaner Beaner, poor Rat Zakary. They were like two chickens in the rain. They made their slow way to the park bench, dripping and freezing, and thinking about their day. "Rats," said the Meaner. "The junkyard dog bit my rear end, and we fell in McGreggor's Creek...BUT AT LEAST I DON'T HAVE TO WRITE THAT SSSSSTUPID POP TEST!" Nyuk, nyuk, nyuk. Chidder, chidder, chidder, went Zakary.

Rat Zakary was not happy. He ran over to a sunny stone, lay down, and went to sleep. Skipping school was not for him. The Meaner Beaner sat on a park bench and looked around. Seagulls were flying like kites in the blue sky. Chipmunks were scurrying up trees. Friendly garter snakes were slithering down to McGreggor's Creek. The Meaner lay back on the park bench and closed his eyes, letting the warm sun dry his clothes. Then, suddenly, something dropped from the sky and landed, SPLAT, on the Meaner's forehead. He opened his eyes and spied a sea gull high in the sky, directly over his head.

"AAAAUUUUGGGGGGHHHHHHH," the Meaner howled so loud that Zakary was bolted from the stone. The Meaner raced down to McGreggor's Creek to wash the gooey bird plop from his hair.

The Meaner once again thought about his day. "The junkyard dog bit my rear end, we fell in McGreggor's Creek, and a bird plopped on my head...BUT AT LEAST I DON'T HAVE TO WRITE THAT SSSSSTUPID POP TEST!" Nyuk, nyuk, nyuk, went the Meaner, and the unhappy rat said nothing.

The afternoon sun was crossing the sky and the dastardly duo were getting hungry. The Meaner reached into his pocket and pulled out the perfect lunch for Rat Zakary—a beautiful orange and black monarch butterfly. Zakary ate the butterfly in one chomp—it was SOOOOOO DELICIOUS. But the Meaner's tummy wanted something different, so with Zakary on his shoulder, he walked over to Jimmi Ho's Chinese General Store. Jimmi Ho was surprised to see the Meaner and his pet rat. "Mr. William, why are you not at school today?"

"Well, um, well...you see...well, it's a PD day today, Jimmi Ho," the Meaner stammered.

"A PD Day? That is very strange. I have not seen any other kids in my store today. Are you sure it is a PD day, Mr. William?"

"Well, yes, I am, Jimmi Ho. I really should know if it is a PD day, shouldn't I?...Anyway, I would like to buy a chocolate bar. Do you have any Chinese Double Star Bars? They are my favorite."

"Well, yes, Mr. William. I have some very fresh Chinese Double Star Bars for $1.00. And over in that box I have some two-week-old Chinese Double Star Bars on sale for 40 cents."

The Meaner thought for a moment. "I think I will buy the forty-cent bar. I don't care if it is not fresh. Chinese Double Star Bars are always good." The Meaner paid for his chocolate bar and walked over to an old bench under a large oak tree. The Meaner's tummy was commanding him: "FEED ME SOME CHINESE DOUBLE STAR BARS, FEED ME SOME CHINESE DOUBLE STAR BARS." The Meaner unwrapped the chocolate bar, closed his eyes, and opened his mouth wide.

He chomped down on the bar, chewed the yummy chocolate slowly, and swallowed. That Double Star Bar was SOOOOOOO GOOD. He opened his eyes, ready for the second chomp. Then—he saw it! There, in the center of the chocolate bar, was one half of a huge, slimy green worm. The other half of the worm, the Meaner instantly knew, was in his stomach. The Meaner began coughing and hacking and spitting. "YYYYUUUUUCKKK," he sputtered and ran to the drinking fountain to wash out the wormy chocolate.

Finally, it was time to make his way towards Brick Street. School would soon be out and he wanted to walk home with all the Brickstreeters so his mom and dad would not know he had skipped school today. "Not the best day," he said to Zakary. "The dog bit my rear end, we fell in the creek, a bird plopped on my head, and I ate a worm. BUT AT LEAST I DIDN'T HAVE TO SIT IN A HOT CLASSROOM AND WRITE A SSSSSTUPID POP TEST!" He gave out one last Meaner chuckle: Nyuk, nyuk, nyuk.

The school bell rang and the kids came running onto the street. "Hey, Meaner, what are you doing here?' asked Joe Ford. "I thought you were sick!" All the kids stood around, gawking at the Meaner Beaner. He looked awful: chocolate was smeared on his face, his shoes were wet and mucky, his hair was caked with white plop, and his polka dot underwear was showing at the back of his pants. Even Rat Zakary looked sad and disheveled.

"Never mind about that," the Meaner said to all the Brickstreeters. "How was YOUR day? HOW DID YOU GOODIE-GOODIES LIKE SITTING IN A HOT, HOT CLASSROOM WRITING A SSSSSTUPID POP TEST?" The Meaner began to laugh at them, "Nyuk, nyuk, nyuk, nyuk, nyuk. At least I didn't have to write a SSSSSTUPID pop test!"

Little Mouse Krause quickly chirped up: "Meaner, what are you talking about? We didn't have a pop test today! Ms. Barnyard took the whole class on a surprise trip to the Ringling Brothers Circus that came for one day to Tin City. We watched wild tigers jump through fiery hoops, and trapeze artists and their amazing jumps, and jugglers juggling swords as sharp as razors. We saw a two-headed dog, a purple cat with three tails, and we laughed and laughed at crazy-weirdo clowns. We had hot dogs, candy apples, caramel corn, and ice cream. It was Ms. Barnyard's special treat – and it was the best day ever!"

"Yeah," the kids all cheered. "IT WAS THE BEST DAY OF THE WHOLE YEAR!"

Poor Meaner stood on the sidewalk, looking like a wilted dandelion. He said nothing and walked away from the Brickstreeters. Then he grumbled and said to his little friend: "There's only one thing worse than getting bird plop on my head—THAT'S WHEN THOSE GOODIE-GOODIES HAVE FUN!!"

And Rat Zakary said nothing at all.

# Chapter Six

## Joy Ride

Tin City was basking in the bright sun. Every Brickstreeter knew it was true—summer was the best time for snatching crayfish from McGreggor's Creek, or climbing the maple trees behind the Scout Hut, or eating giant ice cream cones at Jimmi Ho's Chinese General Store. As the Meaner walked down Dickerson Avenue to the general store, he could almost feel the delicious rainbow-flavored ice cream dripping from his tongue.

Passing by Poppy Morgan's tomato field on the hill, he noticed a little bird sitting on the arm of old Poppy Morgan's scarecrow. The Meaner reached down, picked up a smooth stone from the ground, and threw it with all his might. The stone whizzed through the air, narrowly missing the little bird, scaring it away. Nyuk, nyuk, nyuk, went the Meaner. Walking back to the sidewalk, he trampled on a bed of beautiful red roses in Poppy's garden. Nyuk, nyuk, nyuk, he chuckled again. "THEY DON'T CALL ME THE MEANER BEANER FOR NOTHING."

The Brickstreeters were gathered outside the general store, huddled around Jimmi Ho's brand new Hummer H2. The kids were in awe of the large, wide vehicle. There was not one speck of mud on the tires, nor was there even a whiff of dust on the inside dashboard. The summer sun shone down on the chrome and the cherry-red paint, and Jimmi Ho's new Hummer gleamed like a polished penny.

The Meaner walked by the Brickstreeters and the Hummer, not bothering to look up. The goodie-goodies were having fun—and that pained him more than a thousand mosquito bites.

58 Robert Harry Kerr

Inside Jimmi Ho's Chinese General Store, Frannie and Sadie were licking their giant ice cream cones. "Hey, Meaner," said Frannie, "did you see Jimmi Ho's new Hummer H2 outside? It's as shiny as a polished penny."

The Meaner glared at the girls. "Do you know what would look nice on that Hummer?" he whispered to them.

"What?" they asked.

"Bird plop," said the Meaner Beaner. "That Hummer is way too shiny. It looks SSSSSTUPID. What that big Hummer-car needs is some pearly white bird plop."

"YUCK!," said the two girls at once. "That is GROSS! How can we eat giant ice-cream cones when you talk about bird plop?"

Nyuk, nyuk, nyuk, went the Meaner.

That night Joe Ford phoned the Meaner. "Hey Meaner," said Joe, "are you going to the Night Party at Brick Lake next weekend ? Mayor Nancy will be there, and we will be having a campfire with roasty wieners and toasty marshmallows. The mayor says this is going to be the BEST NIGHT PARTY IN THE HISTORY OF BRICK LAKE "

"Night Parties are for PINHEADS," said the Meaner and he hung up the phone on Joe Ford. The Meaner Beaner put on his nightmare pajamas, turned out the light, and walked over to the cage of his best buddy, Rat Zakary.

"Hello little friend," he whispered. "Next weekend is going to be very bad. The Brickstreeters are so smiley and happy, because of the Night Party at Brick Lake. They will be roasting wieners and toasting marshmallows and laughing and running around the campfire and chasing fireflies in the night. I HATE WHEN THOSE GOODIE GOODIES HAVE FUN! I gives me a pain in my behind."

Just then, the Meaner picked up Zakary and put him close to his face. Boy to rat. Cheek to cheek. Then, in the deep silence of the room, an idea wormed its way from the rat brain, through Zakary's furry cheek, into the Meaner's fleshy cheek, and up to the Meaner Beaner brain. The rat brain had ZAPPED the human brain. All at once, a smile came to the Meaner's face: "Thank you, little buddy. Thank you for sending to me the dirty little plan. Next weekend, I will caper those goodie-goodies. I will caper them real good. I WILL RUIN THE NIGHT PARTY AT BRICK LAKE." He gave to Zakary his favorite snack: a juicy monarch butterfly.

Saturday night was perfect. An orange moon hung lazily over Brick Lake, the breeze was warm, and a chorus of crickets and frogs filled the night air. Far down Dickerson Avenue, behind Jimmi Ho's Chinese General Store, the Meaner spoke to the little friend perched on his shoulder: "This is a perfect night, Zakary. A perfect night for a joy ride." Nyuk, nyuk, nyuk. Slowly, slowly the Meaner made his way up to the shiny red Hummer. He was carrying his **Secret Box of No-Good Dirty Rotten Tricks.** The Meaner opened the door, hoisted the box onto the passenger seat, and got behind the steering wheel.

Down at Brick Lake the Night Party was roaring, and so was the huge bonfire on the beach. Long sticks poked into the fire, roasting marshmallows and toasting wieners. The kids laughed and sang, and Mayor Nancy told them funny stories. Mayor Nancy was the best mayor in the history of Tin City.

Stuttering Billy Taberham arrived a little late and made an announcement. He told the mayor and all of the people about a strange, strange thing. On his way to B...B...Brick Lake he happened to see J...J...Jimmi Ho's

shiny red Hummer going d...d...down the street – with a
tiny man b...b...behind the steering wheel. And strangest
of all, the tiny man had a b...b...brown rat on his shoulder.
A rat with an extra long t...t...tail. The kids all laughed,
all except Sadie Orson, the worry wart, who said to herself:
"I am worried about this. Very worried."

William Joseph Beaner was cruising down Dickerson
Avenue in Jimmi Ho's new Hummer. He struggled to see
over the steering wheel, and struggled even more to keep
his foot on the gas pedal. The car jerked and bumped, like
it had the hiccups, and it swerved from one side of the road
to the other. "I am a very good driver," he said to Zakary.
"A very good driver." But Zakary's teeth were chattering
like tiny jackhammers.

The Hummer cruised from street to street, all around
Tin City. Just then, the Meaner looked out the side
window. He noticed a skull and cross-bones on a wooden
door. His Meaner brain knew it was true: This must be
Oak Street, the dirtiest, toughest part of town. This was
Freddy Sledgehammer territory! Suddenly, the Meaner hit
the brakes. In the vehicle's headlights he could see
creatures of the night walking towards them. As the
creatures approached the vehicle, the Meaner rolled down
the window. He could see them clearly. It was the
Sledgehammer Gang! The toughest, dirtiest gang of
teenagers in all of Tin City.

Freddy Sledgehammer glared down at the Meaner
Beaner. "Hello Beanbag." Freddy's voice had the sound of
tires spinning on gravel. "Nice Hummer, Beanbag. Very
sharp. Very nifty. Very cool."

The Meaner was a little bit afraid of Freddy. Rat
Zakary was even more afraid. "Th...th...thanks," said the

Meaner, and he could hear Rat Zakary's teeth chattering faster than ever.

"Listen, Beanbag," said Freddy. "We are going over to Jack's Pool Playing Hall on Donner Boulevard tonight. At midnight we will be needing a ride home. Pick us up at the Jack's Pool Playing Hall at midnight. Can you do that?"

S...s...sure," said the Meaner. In the dark night, Freddy looked very scary.

"Good," said Freddy. "If you and the rat can pull this off, we would like you to join the Sledgehammer Gang. We need a guy with a cool Hummer. We need a good-looking rat with sharp fangs and an extra long tail."

The Meaner gave them two thumbs up, Rat Zakary gave them two claws up, and they were off. "At last," said the Meaner, "we will become Sledgehammers! We will not be beanbags anymore. We will be Sledgehammers!" Nyuk, nyuk, nyuk. Chidder, chidder, chidder, went Rat Zakary.

At the corner of King Street and Washington Avenue, the Meaner stopped the Hummer and opened the **Secret Box of No-Good Dirty Rotten Tricks**. He smiled his wicked smile. It was time for CAPER NUMBER ONE. The Meaner pulled something out of the box. Something he had gotten for Christmas last year. It was his High Power, Super-Shot, Goo-Shooter. As the Meaner and Zakary turned onto King Street, he noticed a shadowy character. As the Hummer got closer and closer and closer, the passenger window went down and BOOOO-WAAAANGGGG, the Shooter went off and blasted the shadowy character, head to toe, with yellow, stinking goo. The Meaner laughed so hard, he nearly drove off the road. He rolled down the window and yelled for all the night to hear: "Nyuk, nyuk, nyuk, THEY DON'T CALL ME THE MEANER BEANER FOR NOTHING." Chidder, chidder,

chidder, went Rat Zakary.

"Now it is time for CAPER NUMBER TWO," said the Meaner, and he drove the Hummer back to Oak Street, back to the dark, dark alley beside the Sledgehammer clubhouse. He stopped the Hummer. He waited. All was quiet. Suddenly, the Meaner blew the horn three times, long and loud. In the blink of an eye, fifty alley dogs tore onto the street, barking wildly and biting the tires of the Hummer. The Meaner laughed loudly and spun the tires. The Hummer shot down the road like a bullet. The alley dogs chased after the car, howling and barking and biting at the back tires—just what the Meaner wanted! Rat Zakary closed his red eyes, thinking he would be surely eaten by an alley dog. Faster and faster the Meaner drove the Hummer, and he swerved madly from one side of the road to the other. The Hummer made the turn back onto King Street. The fifty dogs made the turn, barking and snarling and biting more angrily than ever.

The Hummer turned onto Donner Boulevard, the dogs turned onto Donner Boulevard, and Zakary could not open his tiny red eyes. The zooming Hummer made a hairpin turn at Huckleberry and another hairpin turn onto Brick Street, and the speeding car was now aimed directly at the beach of Brick Lake. The Meaner chuckled, Nyuk, nyuk, nyuk. The alley dogs would soon be destroying the party. They would be chasing and biting those wiener-roasting, marshmallow-toasting goodie-goodies. Yes, yes, he was going to RUIN the Night Party at Brick Lake. Nyuk, nyuk, nyuk.

Down at Brick Lake, Sadie Orson looked up from the campfire. She stopped eating her toasty marshmallow. She heard something coming down the road. "I am very worried about this," she said to herself. "Very worried."

Suddenly, everyone heard the noise, and they stopped eating their wieners and marshmallows. When they looked far down Brick Street, they could not believe their eyes! Jimmi Ho's shiny red Hummer H2 was going 100 miles per hour with a miniature driver behind the wheel and fifty barking, snarling, biting dogs in pursuit.

"AAAAAAAAAAAAAAAAAHHHHHHHH," the kids all screamed. "It's the alley dogs from Oak Street! The meanest, growlingest, bitingest dogs in Tin City! We will all become dog food!" Just then, Toby the cat flew out of Naj Singh's arms. As the Hummer streaked past the camp fire, the alley dogs veered off and chased the cat. Toby ran down Brick Street with the dogs snarling and barking and wanting to bite the delicious cat. Toby the cat cut across the T...T...Taberham lawn. The dogs cut across the T...T...Taberham lawn. Toby jumped Joe Ford's high fence. The fifty dogs jumped Joe Ford's high fence. Toby turned sharply, ran through backyards all the way to Lincoln Avenue, and darted up the steps of a large, large building. The alley dogs turned sharply, ran through backyards all the way to Lincoln Avenue, and darted up the steps of the large, large building. Inside the dark building, the dogs stopped. For an instant all was quiet. Very, very quiet. Suddenly, a large door clanked shut. The fifty dogs were trapped behind steel bars. Toby, the smartest cat in Tin City, had taken them to Pets' Jail.

Back inside the Hummer, the Meaner reached into his **Secret Box of No-Good Dirty Rotten Tricks** and pulled out a can of jet-black paint. He got out of the Hummer. Slowly, carefully, the Meaner poured the paint on the side of the road, making a huge black puddle right beside the sidewalk. The Meaner drove down the road, stopped the Hummer and waited. "The Night Party is almost over," he told Zakary. "When those goodie-goodies make their way down Brick Street, it will be time for CAPER NUMBER THREE."

It was Rat Zakary who first noticed them. Seven or eight kids, making their way down the sidewalk. The walkers were whistling and talking and had no idea what was about to happen to them. Chidder, chidder, chidder, went Rat Zakary. Nyuk, nyuk, nyuk, went the Meaner. They could hardly wait.

As the kids walked closer to the black puddles, the Hummer started up and zoomed towards them. The Hummer hit the puddle at full speed and, SPLAAAAAAAAAASH, a mountainous wave of jet-black paint washed the sidewalkers head to toe, every one. The Hummer raced far down the road, and the Meaner and Zakary could hear them yelling nineteen-letter swear words. In the rear-view mirror the Meaner could see the kids, dripping with black paint and shaking their fists into the air. CAPER NUMBER THREE had been so much fun, and the two criminals laughed and laughed: Nyuk, nyuk, nyuk. Chidder, chidder, chidder. For the boy and the rat, this was turning out to be the BEST NIGHT PARTY IN THE HISTORY OF BRICK LAKE!

The Meaner checked his watch. Yikes, it was nearly midnight, time to pick up Freddy and the Sledgehammers at Jack's Pool Playing Hall. The Meaner was very happy with himself as he drove down the road, and he said to his little friend, "Wait until Freddy hears about our wonderful capers, Zakary. The Goo gun. The alley dogs. The jet-black paint. Wait until he finds out that we RUINED THE NIGHT PARTY AT BRICK LAKE. Ruined it for those goodie-goodie Brickstreeters. He will be so happy. He will let us become Sledgehammers." Nyuk, nyuk, nyuk.

Chidder, chidder, chidder.

Just then, the Meaner Beaner heard something. A high-pitched wailing sound. The Meaner knew what it was. A siren. He looked in the rear-view mirror. A flashing red light. "OH, NO, ZAK, IT'S THE SSSSSTUPID COPS! WE ARE IN BIG TROUBLE!" The Meaner tramped the gas pedal to the floor. The Hummer flew down Brick Street and took the corner at Huckleberry on two wheels. The police car raced after the Hummer, down Brick Street, down Huckleberry, straight out of Tin City, down Rikers Road, and, finally, to the end of Pike's Lane. All was dark and quiet as the Hummer came to a dead end.

In front of the Meaner and Zakary and the red Hummer was the worst place in the entire world. The worst place to be on a dark night. The Hummer was stopped on the very edge of the black, stinking waters of the Murky Bog, home of the dreaded Murky Bog Cyclops. Every kid in Tin City knew about the Murky Bog Cyclops, that ugly, hairy, one-eyed monster-man who longed to take children into his watery home. The Meaner's teeth rattled in the night. Zakary's teeth rattled in the night. Suddenly, there came a knock on the side window, but the two criminals were too frightened to look. They were frozen in fear. They could only stare straight ahead. "G...g...go away," stammered the Meaner. We do not want to go with you, Mr. Cyclops. We do not want to go into the Murky Bog with you. G...g...go away." Rat Zakary put his claws over his eyes.

Again there was a knock on the side window and a voice said: "Open the door, little boy, open the door." Slowly, slowly, they turned and looked. It was Officer Bob. They had been caught, but they had been saved.

As the years passed, the people of Tin City would forget many things. But the people of Tin City would never forget this Night Party at Brick Lake. Jimmi Ho would always remember how he had cried and cried when he saw his wonderful Hummer H2, all muddy and scratched and splattered with paint. It was Mayor Nancy who was shot with the goo gun, so much goo in her hair that she had to get buzzed bald. Bald as a chicken egg. She would never forget that bald haircut. Freddy Sledgehammer would never forget how the Beanbag had tricked them, how the Beanbag had raced toward them in the Hummer, coming closer and closer to them, and then hitting the puddle of jet-black paint. Freddy and his whole gang were as black as licorice, and they all swore that the Brick Street kid named William Joseph Beaner and his pet rat would NEVER BECOME SLEDGEHAMMERS, they would ALWAYS BE BEANBAGS! Mr. and Mrs. Beaner would always remember the sad day, two weeks after the Night Party at Brick Lake. It was the day they had to pick up their son AFTER FOURTEEN DAYS IN KIDS' JAIL, and Rat Zakary AFTER FOURTEEN DAYS IN PETS' JAIL.

But who would remember this night the longest? Well, strange as it seems, it would be the Meaner Beaner himself. He would remember forever the one thing that made this night the worst of his life. Of all the terrible things that had happened to him that summer, the most terrible of all was when he heard Joe Ford tell all of the Brickstreeters: "THAT WAS THE BEST NIGHT PARTY IN THE HISTORY OF BRICK LAKE." And all the kids cheered and cheered. His nightmare had once again come true. The pain had come back to his behind. THOSE GOODIE- GOODIES WERE HAVING SO MUCH FUN!

At the end of it all, the 'terrible two' were down—but

they were not done! No, they were never done! They knew
that there would be other parties to caper. Other days to
ruin. In the dim light of the upstairs bedroom, the boy and
the rat stood up straight. The boy put one hand over his
heart, and rat put one claw over his heart. And the Meaner
spoke their mission in life.

Let the Goodies have their good,
Let the Goodies do as they should.
Rotten capers is all we see
Rotten capers they'll get for free
And BAD—that's good enough for Zakary and me!

# Chapter Seven

## The New Neighbor

There was a moving van, as big as a dinosaur, backed in the driveway of 13 Brick Street. The Beaners were getting new next-door neighbors.

William Joseph Beaner was devilishly happy. The Jack family had finally moved out of 13 Brick Street. Nyuk, nyuk, nyuk, said the Meaner. "I pulled so many capers on those Jacks so many times, they finally moved. I guess they didn't like it so much when I chucked rotten eggs at their mangy dog, or when I painted their front lawn orange, or when Rat Zakary ran up Ms. Jack's dress and bit her belly button." Nyuk, nyuk, nyuk.

Now there were new neighbors to caper. With Rat Zakary in his shirt pocket, the Meaner Beaner walked by the moving van. No one was around. The trickster sneaked to the back of the van. He looked left and right on Brick Street—no one around. He knelt beside the huge back tire and whispered, "Get the tire, Zakary, get the tire." Zakary jumped out of the Meaner's pocket and began chewing rubber. When the little rat was done, he gave the new neighbors one last Meaner chuckle: Nyuk, nyuk, nyuk.

When the Meaner Beaner stepped into his own home, he could smell the delicious home-made pizza from the kitchen. "Oh, William," his mother said in a flowery voice, "did you see the moving van next door? Looks like we have new neighbors."

"Oh, yes, Mommy," said the Meaner in his perfect-little-boy voice. "I can hardly wait to meet the new neighbors. I hope they are as nice as the Jack family."

"Me too, Dear. The Jacks were a nice family, but it is

strange how they just up and moved. Hardly said good-bye."

When the Meaner got to his room, he put Rat Zakary back into his cage. He wanted to have a business meeting with his little friend. "Zakary, we have serious work to do, and you are going to have to help me. We need to caper those new neighbors. We need to caper them real good. It will be so much fun."

Chidder, chidder, chidder, went Rat Zakary.

Meaner took Zakary over to his bedroom window and the two friends peered down at 13 Brick Street. The Meaner noticed the new sign on their front porch: **The Deeds Family**. Meaner and Zakary looked towards the big van—with its back tire as flat as a pancake. The Deeds family was there, staring at the flat tire: the father, looking very puzzled, the mother, looking very frustrated, and their pretty daughter, looking very cheery.

Suddenly, the little girl turned her head and looked up at Zakary and Meaner. Zakary and Meaner stared back at the girl, and both of them had crocodile smiles. The smiles seemed to say: Welcome, new neighbor. Welcome to your worst nightmare. The Meaner and Zakary were as happy as two fleas on a dog. But then it happened—the pretty girl smiled back at them! She was not puzzled, like Dad. She was not frustrated, like Mom. She was strangely—and eerily—cheery. As she stared up at Zakary and Meaner, her smile got bigger. It was a smile that seemed to say: Just wait, you little tricksters. Just wait!

Two days later the Meaner was skateboarding down Brick Street, and he stopped in front of his new neighbor's house. Mr. Deeds was in the garage, fixing his motorcycle, and Mrs. Deeds was in the backyard, hanging clothes on the line. Just then, the little girl came out of the house.

She had dark hair, large brown eyes, long eyelashes, and a very pretty face. "Hi," she said to the Meaner. "What's your name?"

"William Joseph Beaner," he said to her, "but the Brickstreeters call me Meaner Beaner. AND THEY DON'T CALL ME THE MEANER BEANER FOR NOTHING. I am the MEANEST kid in Tin City, the rascal of Brick Street, the scamp of the neighborhood, and the worst troublemaker in my class.

"Cool," said the pretty girl. "My name is Nasty. Nasty Deeds. Pleased to meet you."

"Nasty...that's a SSSSTUPID name," scoffed the Meaner. "Your parents must have named you Nasty because you were such an UGLY BABY." The Meaner gave the new girl his famous Meaner chuckle: Nyuk, nyuk, nyuk.

The girl simply shrugged. "That's funny," she giggled.

Funny. The Meaner HATED that. He did not want to be funny. He wanted to be MEAN. "Too bad about the flat tire on your moving-van," he snickered. Then he said, "THEY DON'T CALL ME THE MEANER BEANER FOR NOTHING."

"That's okay," said Nasty Deeds. "Things happen. We got the tire fixed. It's no big deal."

No big deal. The Meaner HATED that also. The flat tire WAS a big deal. It was a wonderfully rotten caper!

"Well," said Nasty, "I've got to go. See you around, William." She then reached out, shook hands with the Meaner, and bounced back into the house.

That night the Beaner tossed and turned. In his nightmares, Nasty Deeds smiled her sweet smile. HE HATED PRETTY GIRLS AND HE HATED SWEET SMILES. Then, at the stroke of midnight, the Meaner

Beaner sat bolt upright in his bed. Zakary's eyes glowed like tiny stoplights in the darkness, and as the Meaner stared back at his little friend, a gloriously evil idea came flying into his Beaner brain. The Meaner climbed out of bed, went over to the rat's cage and said, "Zakary, we have got trouble next door. Trouble—with a capital N and a capital D. I don't trust that kid—she's way too pretty and way too sweet. Almost makes me sick! That Nasty Deeds has to be taught a lesson."

Chidder, chidder, chidder, went Rat Zakary.

In the thick of the night the Meaner Beaner carried Rat Zakary to the downstairs basement, to the Secret Box of No-Good Dirty Rotten Tricks. The Meaner flicked on the light bulb, reached into the box and he pulled out a can of slimy green tobacco worms.

A crescent moon hung lazily in the sky as William Joseph Beaner and Rat Zakary sneaked out their bedroom window, down the television tower, and onto the lawn. More silent than two snakes in the grass, the dastardly duo made their way to the backyard of 13 Brick Street. There they were: Nasty's socks, freshly washed and hanging on the clothesline. The Meaner reached into the blue can, grabbed a fat, slimy tobacco worm, and gave it to Zakary. Zakary jumped onto the clothesline and dropped the worm into a sock. He took another worm and dropped it into another sock. In fifteen minutes, the entire line of socks contained one worm each.

When the caper was done, the tricksters chuckled, nyuk, nyuk, nyuk, and chidder, chidder, chidder, and the Meaner whispered to Zakary: "THEY DON'T CALL ME THE MEANER BEANER FOR NOTHING."

It was late the next afternoon as the Meaner was skateboarding past 13 Brick Street. He noticed Nasty

Deeds coming out of her house. She was carrying a freshly-baked pie and the sweet aroma made him hungry. "Hi, William," she said in a friendly voice.

"The kids call me MEANER," he reminded the pretty girl.

"Oh...that's not very nice of them," she said, winking at him. "I don't think you are mean at all. In fact, I think you are very cute."

The Meaner's face became as red as a fire truck. Cute. That was the worst thing anybody had said to him this year! He HATED cute. He LOVED mean. The Meaner wanted to 'get back' at his new neighbor. "Oh," he said to her, "I just stopped by to warn you about something. We have a big problem with tobacco worms on Brick Street. They love to get into our socks and eat holes." He looked down at her shoes and grinned: "Have you had any trouble with tobacco worms?"

"No problem," she said cheerily. "Besides, I think tobacco worms are cute—just like you, William. Bye now." The girl set the pie on the porch to cool and went back into the house.

The Meaner was becoming frustrated. His blood was boiling. Why didn't the tobacco worms eat holes in her socks? Or was she pretending? Why was she calling him 'William' all the time? Why was she saying he was 'cute' all the time? "This girl needs to learn one thing," he said to himself: "THEY DON'T CALL ME THE MEANER BEANER FOR NOTHING. This new neighbor needs to learn that." The Meaner sneaked up to the porch and snatched the luscious-smelling pie. "Nyuk, nyuk, nyuk," he said as he took off home.

Up in his bedroom, the Meaner's face was green with lime pie. Rat Zakary's fur was green with lime pie. The two

had devoured the delicious green pie that Nasty Deeds had set out to cool. On his last mouthful, the Meaner pronounced: "THERE IS NO SWEETER PIE THAN A SNATCHED PIE," and the two tricksters fell over laughing. Nyuk, nyuk, nyuk. Chidder, chidder, chidder.

The next day the Meaner put on his vampire T-shirt, the one that made some of the kindergarten kids cry. He ran to the basement and opened his **Secret Box of No-Good Dirty Rotten Tricks** and retrieved a giant plastic tulip and pinned it to his T-shirt.

After a quick breakfast he was once again outside, skateboarding the sidewalks of Brick Street. Down at Brick Street Park he did a couple of ollies, a few grinds, and a three-sixty. He rattled his way towards home, passing his new neighbor's house. Nasty Deeds was outside flying a kite. The Meaner left his skateboard on the sidewalk and came over to her. "Hey, Deeds," he said in a sarcastic voice, "How was your green pie? Did you have it for supper last night? Was it good?"

"Oh, hi William," said the pretty girl. "No, we ended up going out to a restaurant last night. For dessert I had apple crisp with double ice cream. That was better than green pie...Hey, I like your vampire T-shirt. Nice tulip, can I smell it?" The girl put her nose to the giant flower and then all at once, ZAAAAAAAAAAAAAAAAAAAPO, Rat Zakary jumped out, onto her nose, down her shirt, down her pants, back up her leg and arm and became buried in the girl's long hair.

The girl lifted the rat out of her hair and looked at it. She began giggling and giggling. "It's a SWEET little pet. He looks so CUTE with his extra long tail," she said.

Sweet little pet. Cute with his extra long tail. The Meaner's teeth began to grind. Zakary's teeth began to grind. Rats are NOT sweet! They are NOT cute! They are CREEPY and TERRIFYING! Definitely not cute! Zakary and Meaner HATED that word more than they had ever hated any word. This girl was becoming impossible! As they walked back home, the Meaner could think of only one thing: That Deeds girl will learn it sooner or later: They don't call me the Meaner Beaner for nothing!

That night, up in his room, the Meaner was in his favorite nightmare pajamas, feeding Zakary a monarch butterfly, when his mother knocked on his door. "William," she said, "your father and I are taking a trip tomorrow. We are going to Niagara Falls very early, and we are going to leave you alone for the morning. We will be back in the afternoon."

"Oh, that's okay, Mummy. I won't really be alone. Zakary will be here with me."

"Yes, of course," said Mrs. Beaner. "Oh, one more thing. I was downstairs and I noticed something very surprising. As I was looking out the kitchen window, I noticed a moving van at 13 Brick Street. It seems that our new neighbors are moving out...That is strange. They have only been here a few days, and now they are moving. I wonder why."

When Mrs. Beaner left, the Meaner went over to Zakary's cage. "Hooooooooray, hoooooooray, hoooooooray," the Meaner said to Zakary. "The Deeds are moving. Yowzer, yowzer, yowzer, our dirty capers made them move. Finally, that Deeds girl knows it is true: They don't call me the Meaner Beaner for nothing." Nyuk, nyuk, nyuk, went the Meaner. Chidder, chidder, chidder, went Rat Zakary. It was a happy, happy day for the 'terrible two.'

That night the Meaner slept like a pig in mud. He had the best dreams ever. He dreamt that he was playing grand capers on the Deeds family, and Nasty Deeds was yelling and whining at his tricks, and at the end of the dream she was screaming at him and calling him the worst trickster in the history of Brick Street. In the dream, Nasty Deeds told him that he was NOT cute, and that Zakary was NOT cute. She was screaming at them, telling them how HORRIBLE and ROTTEN they were. It was the best dream he had ever had.

But the next morning was nothing like a good dream. At six o'clock in the morning a loud siren went off in the Beaner house. The Meaner bolted upright in his bed, hitting his head on a water balloon. The balloon burst and completely soaked his bed, pillow and nightmare pajamas. The siren was still wailing as the Beaner stepped out of bed, instantly slipping on the bedroom floor. The entire bedroom floor was knee-high in chocolate pudding, and he continued to slip and slide all the way over to his closet. He was a complete mess as he opened the closet door, and there, staring at him, with a cracked skull and blood-red eyes, was a horrific smiling skeleton: The Meaner cried out in the dim room, "AAAAAUUUUUGGGHHHHHHH," and Rat Zakary shivered like a leaf in a storm. In giant, galloping leaps the Meaner made his way out of the chocolate-pudding room, straight into the washroom, into the bathtub, and quickly turned on the shower. It came streaming out of the shower—not the nice warm water he was used to every morning—but gooey, spicy spaghetti sauce. His hair, face, arms, legs and bum were orange with spaghetti sauce and the Meaner now smelled like an Italian restaurant. Again he yelled out: "AAUGGGGHHH." The Meaner jumped out of the tub, grabbed a towel, and frantically began wiping the spaghetti sauce off his body. But he suddenly realized the towel was stitched with

sandpaper and the Meaner's arms and legs and bum were
scratched as red as a cherry. "AAAAAUUUUGGGHHH,"
the Meaner wailed. The siren was still blaring and he
knew he had to get out of here. He pulled on his shirt, a
pair of jeans and reached for a pair of socks on the counter.
He quickly yanked the socks on, and then a whelping pain
came to his toes and he yelled out, "AAAAAUUUGGGGG."
He whipped off the socks and twenty crayfish fell to the
floor. He ran for the stairs, stepped once, slipped, and
rolled like a barrel all the way to the bottom: each stair
had been plastered with axle grease.

Suddenly the siren stopped. The place was now quiet.
With his toes stinging from the crayfish bites, the Meaner
limped across the kitchen floor, over to the refrigerator. He
needed breakfast, but when he opened the fridge door, he
saw only one item of food: one, little chicken egg. He got
out a frying pan and cracked the egg open. The Meaner
could not believe his eyes. When he cracked the shell, out
jumped a baby alligator. The little gator scurried up his
arm and chomped down hard on the Meaner's nose:
"AAAAAAAUUUUGGGGGHHHHHH," the Meaner
yelped. The Meaner could take it no longer—he ran outside
into the cool morning air. He grabbed his skateboard and
jumped on. He had to get far away from here. But the
skateboard instantly collapsed and the Meaner fell flat on
the sidewalk. Looking at the skateboard, he could see that
the wheels had been replaced by Oreo cookies. The day
was worse than a bad dream.

As the Meaner lay on the sidewalk, his feet were slimy
with pudding, his body smelled of spaghetti sauce, his bum
was sore from the sandpaper, his toes ached from crayfish
bites, and his nose was cherry-red from the alligator bite.
Just then, the mailman came up. "Meaner," he said, "you

look awful—and you smell like an Italian restaurant. Here," he said, handing the Meaner a letter, "this is for you. I hope it cheers you up."

The Meaner sat up and opened the letter. It said these words.

**Dear William,**

Sorry I did not say good-bye, but my dad got a new job and we had to move to New York City. I still think you are cute. I think your furry little rat is very cute. Did you have fun this morning? I hope so. Whenever you think of me, just remember this:
THEY DON'T CALL ME NASTY DEEDS FOR NOTHING.

P.S. I hope you and Rat Zakary enjoyed my Tobacco Worm Pie!

# Chapter Eight

## The P...P...Pool Party

Can bad things happen to good people? Yes, everybody knows it's true. Everybody has some bad luck once in a while. And, it doesn't matter how good you are, how kind you are, how polite you are—anybody can have a freakish accident. A freakish accident is very bad luck! There was a good boy who lived in Tin City, and one day he had some very bad luck. It was a freakish accident for sure—and it all began on the hottest day in the history of Tin City.

In mid August Tin City was cooking under a yellow sun. The sidewalks were like stove tops and the beach at Brick Lake was like an oven. Jimmi Ho told all of the Brickstreeters that these were the "dog days of summer"— way too hot to play soccer, way too hot to wash the dog, way too hot to chew gum. But these days were perfect, Jimmi Ho told them, for eating giant ice cream cones. And that's what they did. The kids of Tin City came down to Jimmi Ho's Chinese General Store with their one-dollar bills and feasted on ice cream that burned their teeth cold: Butterscotch Ripple, Chocolate Sunshine, Cookie Crumble, Lickity Split, Jungle Jam, Rainbow Raisin, Lollipop Lemon-Lime, Strawberry Fudge, Chinese Fireworks and Banana Kazam.

When Stuttering Billy Taberham finished his giant B...B...Blueberry B...B...Bonanza ice cream cone, he made his way to the Beaner house at 11 Brick Street and knocked three times. "Oh, hello, Billy," said Ms. Beaner. It is way too hot to be knocking on the door, please come in."

Billy stepped inside. "Thank you, Ms. B...B...Beaner. Is

81

the M...M...Meaner home? I would like to invite him to my p...p...pool party tomorrow afternoon."

Ms. Beaner smiled sweetly. "Oh, Billy, that is so thoughtful. William loves to spend time with all of his good friends. I think he is upstairs in his room. Why don't you go up and invite him yourself?"

Billy trudged up the stairs and walked down the long hallway. He stopped in front of the Meaner's bedroom door and knocked gently. There was no answer. All was quiet. Billy opened the door and the room was as dark and quiet as a cave. He spoke in a low voice: "M...M...Meaner. Are you h...h...here?' Again there was no answer and all was still in the dark room.

Just then, Billy noticed a light from one corner of the dark bedroom. Actually...no...there were two lights. Two tiny, shiny, red, pinhole-dots of light. Once again Billy whispered, "M...M...Meaner. Is that you? Are you here?" He heard only one sound—a small chidder. He wondered to himself: Is that devilish Meaner B...B...Beaner playing a dirty c...c...caper on me?"

Stuttering Billy walked to the corner of the room and stopped in front of the lights. He stared at those lights, eyes wide open, not blinking once. A small chidder once again broke the silence. And then, in the blink of an eye, it happened. ZZZZZZZZZZZZAAAAAAAAAAP. A tremendous flash of electricity lit up the room, snaked its way up from the red lights, through the darkness, and hit Billy Taberham square in his stuttering brain. It was an accident all right, but Billy Taberham had been truly zapped.

Billy walked under the hot sun towards his own home. He felt very strange. As he walked along, he noticed a white cat coming towards him. It was a cute, furry little cat and when the little animal saw Billy, it smiled and began to purr gently. Billy looked at the white cat, and he reached down and picked up a stone. He then threw the stone at the little animal, nicking it on the tail. The good cat turned mad and screeched at Billy; it hissed at him; it wanted to bite him. Billy looked the cat square in the eye and he went, "Nyuk, nyuk, nyuk." And not one stutter did he make.

The next day, Tuesday, was hotter than ever—a truly great day for Stuttering Billy's p...p...pool party. When the sun was at its highest point in the afternoon sky, the Brickstreeters made their way to Billy Taberham's backyard. The first to arrive was Sadie Orson, the worry wart, along with her kindergarten brother, Todd. Sadie was always worried, and today was no different. "There is going to be trouble at the party, I just know it."

The other kids came in, worrying about nothing at all. Annabelle Jefferson brought her alligator floatie and wore her favorite crocodile swimsuit. Louie Gomez and Naj Singh came in together, looking very cool indeed in their matching Ray Ban sunglasses. Little Mouse Krause brought a giant red and white beach ball and Frannie O'Neill lugged in a one-person, green sailboat. The genius dog, Pavlov, came into the backyard with his pet boy, Jeremy, who was not very smart but very kind and very polite.

At three o'clock in the afternoon, Goose Anderson came through the backyard gate and all the kids together let out one huge gasp. Goose had brought a special guest to the party, all ready for a swim in the Taberham p...p...pool. It was his pet pig, Oink. "NOOOOOOOOOOOO," the kids all yelled at once. "Don't let Oink in the pool! Pigs do DISGUSTING THINGS when they are in the pool!" And so

Oink the Pig had to be tied to the back fence. He was not happy.

By two o'clock the kids began to wonder: Where is the Meaner Beaner? They knew that Billy had gone over to Meaner's house to invite him—so why was he not at the p...p...pool party? They were getting very suspicious: Were the Meaner and Zakary up in Taberham's oak tree, spying on them? Were they hiding behind some bushes, getting ready to throw something slimy on them? Were they in the deep end of the pool, holding their breath, acting like sharks, waiting to bite their little toes? Where were the 'terrible two,' anyway? Sadie, the worry wart, said to them all: "The Meaner and Zakary are going to attack the p...p...pool party, I just know it!"

By mid afternoon, one hundred kids were in stuttering Billy Taberham's backyard, splashing, yelling, laughing, running, jumping and singing. The kids drank pop, ate hot dogs, dived into the deep end of the p...p...pool and played games of tag and Red Light on the green grass. When the games of tag and Red Light were done, Pavlov entertained them all with wonderful magic tricks that he had learned from the internet. At one point, he made Todd Orson, the kindergarten kid, disappear. Sadie worried greatly about this, but then, in a puff of smoke, Todd re-appeared on the diving board of the pool and Sadie smiled with relief. Her little brother was safe.

What a splendid day it was! The kids laughed and sprayed each other with the garden hose, and the Meaner Beaner and Rat Zakary were no where to be seen. Perhaps they had gone to Miami for the weekend, or to Detroit, or to the North Pole. It was a marvelous, marvelous day and every Brickstreeter thought the same thing: THIS IS THE BEST P...P...POOL PARTY IN THE HISTORY OF TIN

CITY. Even Sadie Orson had stopped worrying about terrible things that might happen, and she told all of her friends in the pool: "The Meaner and Zakary have gone away for the weekend. There is nothing to worry about. Nothing at all."

The kids were having the time of their lives, yes, but there was one who was not. Oink the Pig, tied to the back fence, baking under the hot sun, looked at the lovely, lovely p...p...pool of blue water. He was still not happy.

Just then, above all the noise and commotion, there was the shrieking sound of a whistle. The kids all stopped and listened. There, standing on the diving board, was the leader of the party, Billy Taberham. He stood up tall and made an announcement to all the kids.

"Boys and girls, thank you for coming to my pool party. You Brickstreeters are the best kids in Tin City. I hope you are having a wonderful time. I hope you are eating all the hot dogs you can eat and drinking all the pop you can drink. And, I hope you are enjoying the mighty magic of our good friend, Pavlov. Have fun, Brickstreeters. Stay as late as you want. Be as messy as you want. I want this to be the BEST POOL PARTY IN THE HISTORY OF TIN CITY."

When Billy finished his speech, the entire backyard became as quiet as a church. The kids could hardly believe their ears. It was a good speech...actually, a great speech...actually, a perfect speech! Yes, Billy had made a perfect speech and not one stutter did he make. Not one single 'p' was stuttered, not one single 'd,' not one single 'w.' It was a miracle—Stuttering Billy was no longer stuttering. Suddenly, Naj Singh began clapping his hands, then Goose Anderson joined in, then Marjorie Kell and Mouse Krause, then Louie Gomez and the pet boy, Jeremy.

In a few seconds every Brickstreeter was clapping and clapping and clapping. They were clapping for Billy Taberham's perfect un-stuttering speech.

Standing on the diving board, Billy bowed respectfully and, in a perfect voice, said to them, "Thank you, Brickstreeters, thank you." And, once again, not one stutter did he make. He said to them all: "Enjoy the pool party." And then a smile came to his face. This was not the sweet, innocent smile that Billy always smiled. No, this was not a Billy Taberham smile, it was more the smile of a lizard, or a snake, or a bad, bad boy.

Pavlov began thinking very hard. His genius brain told him that something very, very strange was happening at this pool party. The good boy, Billy Taberham, was smiling like a bad boy—why was that? Billy was not stuttering any more—why was that? The Meaner Beaner was not at the p...p...pool party—why was that? Things did not make sense to Pavlov's scientific brain. Things did not compute. Things were not right!

At three o'clock in the afternoon Billy Taberham came out of his house, carrying a large brown bottle. He set the bottle on a lawn table and put up a sign for all to see.

> ## FREE SUNTAN OIL

The kids all rushed over to the table and formed a long line. It was a hot, hot day, and suntan oil was just what they needed. Billy Taberham was such a great guy! Billy helped the kids put the gooey oil on their arms and legs and backs. Frannie put extra oil on her freckle face. Louie Gomez had the shortest haircut in Tin City and he gooped it on top of this head and around his ears. Little Todd Orson squished the oil between his toes and Marjorie Kell splashed it under her arms and on her pink nose. The pet boy, Jeremy, rubbed the oil all over his white body and behind his ears. Goose Anderson filled a pail with Billy's suntan oil and brushed it all over his good friend, Oink the Pig. Still, Oink was not happy. He did not like being tied to the back fence, and he wanted to jump into that pool. In twenty minutes every kid was lathered up with Billy Taberham's suntan oil. Pavlov noticed that Billy was still smiling like a lizard, and so the genius dog chalked "no thanks" to the suntan oil.

All at once, a low dark cloud appeared in the sky. The cloud came closer and closer, and it became bigger and bigger. Sadie Orson pointed to the sky and cried out, "Look at that big, ugly cloud. It is going to rain on our party!" As the kids all looked up at the dark cloud, their mouths open wide, Pavlov scribbled a message on his chalkboard and he showed them all: **This is not a cloud of rain.** And then he scribbled one more message for them all to see: **This is a cloud of Flying Spider Beetles.**

Pavlov was right. The cloud of Flying Spider Beetles came down on the party, landing on arms and ears and legs and backs and noses and toes and elbows and freckles. Some of the Spider Beetles landed on Louie Gomez's shaved head and some landed on Oink the Pig. Ten thousand Spider Beetles chased the kids around the backyard, landing on them, pinching them everywhere. The pool partiers all screamed in pain, AAAAAUUHHHH, and Sadie Orson cried out, "I hate Spider Beetles, I hate Spider Beetles." At the back fence, Oink the Pig squealed in pain: OOORRRRRRRREEEEEEEEE. All at once the kids jumped into the swimming pool, held their breath, and dived deep under the water.

In five minutes the Flying Spider Beetles were gone

and the kids all looked at the genius dog. He was the only one who had not been stung. Not one bite did Pavlov receive. "What happened, Pavlov, what happened?" To answer their question, Pavlov scribbled three words on his chalkboard: **Your suntan oil**. And then he scribbled two more words: **was laced**. And then three last words: **with hot pepper**. They put the words together: **Your suntan oil was laced with hot pepper.**

Mouse Krause yelled it out first: "Billy tricked us! He put hot pepper in the suntan oil—and Flying Spider Beetles love hot pepper! We learned that in science class!" The kids gritted their teeth in anger and they looked around for Billy Taberham, but he was no where to be seen. Once again Mouse yelled out: "Let's find that no-stuttering Billy Taberham and throw him in the pool!"

But before the kids could make a move, something happened. The back yard was suddenly filled with a watery-watery mist. One hundred lawn sprinklers came on, all at once, spraying the entire backyard. The kids plugged their noses and shut their eyes as the spray hit their bodies, and when they opened their eyes they were left in shock. Their bodies had turned purple. Julie Fonzio was purple, head to toe. Frannie's freckles were purple, Mouse's pigtails were purple, Oink the Pig was purple, Louie's bald head was purple, the grass was purple, the diving board was purple, and Todd Orson, the kindergarten kid, looked like a grape. Sadie, the worry-wart, yelled out, "I hate purple, I hate purple," and once again the pool partiers all screamed, AAAAAAHHHHHH.

Just then, Oink the purple Pig, let out an ear-piercing squeal, OOOORRRREEEEEEEEEEEEEEEEEEE, and he bolted wildly up into the air. The rope around his neck broke and Oink took off like a big fat rocket. The purple pig ran around the pool at full speed, knocking over tables of pop, knocking over the barbecue and all of the hot dogs, knocking over Billy's Suntan Stand, and knocking little Todd Orson flat on his bum. Todd began whining and crying, "I want to go home, I want to go home, I hate purple pigs, WWAAAAAAAAAAAAAAAAAAAAAAAAAAAA."

Above all the clamor and commotion, Goose Anderson yelled as loudly as he could: "Oink is going crazy. Oink is going crazy. Quick, everybody, get out of his way. Jump back in the pool!" And then, one by one, or two by two, or three by three, they all jumped back into the pool.

When every kid was back in the pool, the purple pig stopped running. He stopped going crazy. Oink looked at all of the kids in the cool, beautiful, blue water. They were laughing and splashing and diving deep. They were having such a wonderful time. Oink backed up all the way to the fence. He stopped and took one last look at all the happy, splashing kids – AND THEN HE RAN! The purple pig ran for all he was worth. He hit the diving board at 100 miles per hour and sprang high into the air, higher than the Taberham's tall oak tree, and once again the kids all screamed: AAAAAAAAAAAAAAAAAAHHHHHHHHHHHH.

Oink, the big, fat, purple Pig, hit the water like a giant cannon ball, and a great splash rose from the pool. It was the BIGGEST SPLASH IN THE HISTORY OF TIN CITY. Oink was now in the pool with the kids and he was soooooooooooooooo happy. The water was cool and beautiful, and Oink loved playing water games with the kids. He held his breath, dived deep and shot up from the pool like an ocean whale. He played Ocean Tag and Water Ball with the kids, and he jumped off the diving board fifty more times. This was Oink's happiest day.

Then, it happened. Louie Gomez noticed it first. "Look,

everybody, look!" And the kids all looked. There was a cloud of water forming in the middle of the pool. It was a yellowish-greenish-brownish cloud—and it was growing and growing and growing. And then they noticed something else. A terrible, terrible smell rose up from the pool—a smell far worse than a cow's back end, far worse than a bag of rotten potatoes, far worse than a ten-day-old dead skunk. IT WAS THE WORSE STINK IN THE HISTORY OF TIN CITY.

For the third time today, the kids all screamed, AAAAAAAAAAAAHHHHHHHH, and Annabelle Jefferson yelled, "Oink has done A DISGUSTING THING in the pool. Quick, get out, get out, get out!" And the kids clamored to get out of the pool. They grabbed their towels and hats and sunglasses and they tore out of the backyard. They ran down Brick Street, every one, and they did not stop running until they got home. Once they got home, every Brickstreeter took a one-hour shower, with extra soap, extra shampoo, and extra body oil.

Back at the Taberham's, all was quiet. Billy walked slowly out of his house and into the backyard. The entire place was a complete a mess. The barbecue was broken and hot dogs were on the grass. Chairs were turned over and tables were smashed, and everything was purple. Billy stood in silence and looked at all the mess, and he thought about his pool party. He remembered the peppered suntan oil and the Flying Spider Beetles. He remembered the water sprinklers that turned all the kids purple, and he remembered Oink the Pig running around the pool and chasing the kids. He remembered the water turning yellowish-greenish-brown, and he remembered the terrible, terrible smell that came up from the pool. Oink had done a DISGUSTING THING in the pool, and the kids had their day ruined. They ran home whining and crying and yelling and screaming. It was their worst day! Once again a twinkle came to Billy Taberham's eye, a snake-like smile came to his face, and he began laughing: Nyuk, nyuk, nyuk. Nyuk, nyuk, nyuk. Nyuk, nyuk, nyuk.

The next day, the Brickstreeters were standing outside Jimmi Ho's Chinese General Store. It was another hot day, but the kids had no money for ice cream. In a little while they noticed a boy coming down the sidewalk, and as he got closer, they knew that it was Billy Taberham. Billy did not say hi to the kids and the kids did not say hi to Billy. No one said anything at all as Billy walked into Jimmi Ho's Store.

In five minutes Billy came out of the store carrying a large box. He set the box down and said to the kids, "I g...g...got you g...g...guys some p...p...popsicles. It is a very hot d...d...day." And then he handed them cold popsicles of every kind: chocolate swirl, raspberry riot, lemon sunshine, orange delight, frosty mint, purple penguin and many more. The kids licked their cold-cold popsicles on this hot-hot day.

When they were done the popsicles, Mouse Krause stepped up to Billy and said, "Thank you Billy. Those popsicles were soooooooooo good. And do you know what else?"

"W...w...what?" asked Billy.

"We like you a lot better when you stutter." And the kids laughed and laughed and laughed—even Billy Taberham.

# Chapter Nine

## The Trip to New Zoo

The summertime of Tin City flew by, faster than ever. September was here—the time for backpacks, freshly sharpened pencils, and the smell of new shoes. It was the first week of school. Back to reality.

On the first Friday of school Mrs. Barnyard had a special announcement for her class. "Well, children, Brick Street School has just been told that New Zoo has finally opened.

"YEEEEAAAAAHHH!" the class yelled wildly.

"At last, at last," shouted Julie Fonzio. "At last we have a zoo in Tin City. Now we are just like Miami and Cincinnati and Chicagee.'

"And," said stuttering Billy Taberham, "we are just like S...S...San Franciscee."

"Yes, yes we are," said Mrs. Barnyard. "And now for the big surprise: Our class has been chosen to be the first school visitors to New Zoo. We will be taking the bus on Monday morning. Big Mr. Little will be our bus driver."

Once again the class cheered wildly. They could hardly believe the good news. They would be the very first class to go to New Zoo. They would ride the bus, and they would be going with their favorite bus driver in the whole world, Big Mr. Little. Mouse Krause danced on top of her desk, Joe Ford yelped like a hyena and Goose Anderson howled like a baboon. Naj Singh, Joe Ford and Louie Gomez went to the head of the classroom, threw their arms into the air, and shouted out a cheer:

Monkeys, mynahs, rhinos too
Lions and tigers at the zoo,

Pythons, boas, rattlers too
Chimps and zebras at the zoo
Five, four, three and two,
It's off on Monday to the zoo.
Five, four, three and two,
It's off on Monday to the zoo.


The kids all clapped along as Naj, Joe and Louie sang their cheer over and over, and Mrs. Barnyard danced a jig. It was the best Friday in the history of Brick Street School.

Finally, the class had calmed down, and Sadie Orson raised her hand. Sadie could not help being the worry wart. "Mrs. Barnyard, I am worried. Big Mr. Little is very strong but he is not very smart. He does not know how to find New Zoo. We will get lost."

The kids all looked up at Mrs. Barnyard. "No need to worry, Sadie. New Zoo has sent us a map. I have put it in a red envelope on my desk. Big Mr. Little will follow the map all the way to New Zoo, no problem."

"Well, okay," said Sadie, but she still looked worried.

Making their way home, the Brickstreeters were filled with joy. The trip to New Zoo would be the BEST FIELD TRIP IN THE HISTORY OF BRICK STREET SCHOOL! The Meaner, a mile behind the rest, kicked a stone all the way down the sidewalk. "School trips are for PINHEADS!" he griped to himself, as foul as a barnyard rooster. "SSSSSTUPID TRIP, SSSSSTUPID ZOO, SSSSSTUPID YELLOW BUS." It was a truly gray day for the Meaner Beaner. On Monday the Brickstreeters would be riding the bus and laughing and cheering and having fun—and the thought of all that was giving the Meaner a pain in his behind.

When the Meaner got to 11 Brick Street, he kicked

open the front door, dropped his school bag on the floor, tramped his dirty boots all the way upstairs, and slammed the bedroom door so loud it shook the windows. Rat Zakary was in his cage, chewing on a monarch butterfly. Chidder, chidder, chidder, went Zakary. He loved monarch butterflies. The Meaner told his furry friend the bad news: "We are having a NO GOOD TRIP on Monday, Zakary...A no-good trip to New Zoo. Big Mr. Little is going to be our bus driver and that is making the Brickstreeters even happier...They were laughing all the way home today...I HATE when those soft bellies are so happy!"

In the middle of the night a strange thing happened. William Joseph got out of bed and began sleepwalking. Like a zombie from the grave the Meaner wondered through the blackness to the cage in the corner of the room. There was no light in the room—except the two fiery-red dots that were the tiny eyeballs of Rat Zakary. The rat was not asleep. Even in this black room the furry little animal could see the sleepwalker in his nightmare pajamas. The Meaner stopped in front of the rat cage. Zakary's red-hot eyes stared into the Meaner's eyes, and, suddenly, the sleepwalker began to smile.

"Thank you, little friend, thank you. You have ZAPPED my brain with a very nice, very dirty, little caper. Now I will RUIN THE TRIP TO NEW ZOO. Yes, yes, those Brickstreeters were right—this will be the BEST TRIP IN THE HISTORY OF BRICK STREET SCHOOL," and he gave his little friend a kiss on the whiskers. Chidder, chidder, chidder, went Rat Zakary.

Suddenly the sleepwalker opened his eyes. He knew what he had to do. He went over to his desk and all night long the Meaner Beaner worked on his map to New Zoo. All night he chuckled and chuckled. This would be the map that would ruin the trip to New Zoo. When he was done, the Meaner slipped the paper into a red envelope.

Monday morning was warm and sunny, a perfect day for the trip to New Zoo. As the kids stepped onto the yellow bus, Big Mr. Little greeted them all with a large smile. The kids loved their favorite bus driver and they all brought him a little present. From Frannie O'Neill he got a four-leave clover. Stuttering Billy Taberham gave his lucky p...p...penny, Pavlov brought a chocolate-flavored dog bone, Annabelle Jefferson gave a dandelion from her lawn, and Mouse Krause gave a lock of hair from her wiener dog, Digger. Big Mr. Little got everything he could ever hope for: a slingshot, three sour apples, a day-old donut, four Chinese Double Star bars, two comic books, an old New York Yankee hat, a Tin City t-shirt, an emu feather, and a green frog. Last on the bus, the Meaner stepped up and gave the bus driver something from his **Secret Box of No-good Dirty Rotten Tricks**—a ball-point pen that exploded ink all over the bus driver when he opened it. The kids all frowned at the dirty trick, but Big Mr. Little laughed and laughed. The Meaner hated that.

The Meaner walked down the aisle of the bus looking for an empty seat. "Hey Meaner," said Joe Ford, "why don't you sit here with me?"

"Because your socks stink," said the Meaner, and he kept walking.

"You can sit beside me," said Julie Fonzio.

"No way," said the Meaner, "I don't want to get the fleas."

When the Meaner passed little Mouse Krause, he said to her: "Hey Krause, I bet the boa constrictor at New Zoo would like you very much—for lunch of course," and he gave her the famous Meaner chuckle: nyuk, nyuk, nyuk.

The kids just smiled and shook their heads. Perhaps Frannie O'Neill was right. Maybe William Joseph Beaner was hatched from a rotten egg. Maybe he was a mean baby. Frannie said that he probably bit his mother as soon as his first tooth came in.

The Meaner moved to the back of the bus where he found a seat all by himself. The Meaner loved the back of the bus. Sitting in the front seat, Mrs. Barnyard handed the red envelope to Big Mr. Little and they were off.

The kids all sang Ninety-nine Bottles of Beer on the Wall and Big Mr. Little drove the yellow bus, carefully following the map in the red envelope. He drove south on Huckleberry, past Tin Can Road and made a left turn onto Riker's Road. "Ms. Barnyard," said the bus driver, scratching his head, "are you sure this is the way to New Zoo?"

"Maps are never wrong, Mr. Little. We learn that in geography class. Trust the map, Mr. Little, trust the map." The yellow bus rattled down Riker's Road, over huge potholes that made the kids bounce off their seats and hit their heads on the tin roof. They rolled past huge boulders that looked like angry gargoyles staring at them. "I'm ever so worried," said Sadie Orson. "Something bad is going to happen, I just know it."

The bus followed Riker's Road into a dark, dangerous forest with trees as high as television towers. Deep in the forest Riker's Road turned to mud and the bus reeled from side to side like a water ski. Sadie Orson began to cry and the Meaner Beaner chuckled in the back seat. "THIS IS THE BEST TRIP I'VE EVER BEEN ON," he mumbled to himself.

Finally, the yellow bus became bogged down, stuck in brown mud that was taller than Mouse Krause. Just then, the kids heard sounds coming from the dark forest. Squealing sounds. The sounds became louder, and the kids could see shadows coming from the trees. The creatures were pink and hairy, with sharp fangs sticking out of their long snouts. The hairy animals came out of the forest and wallowed in the mud all around the yellow bus. Sadie Orson screamed, and all of the kids turned to Pavlov, the best brain on the bus: "WHAT ARE THEY PAVLOV, WHAT ARE THEY?"

Pavlov wrote on his slate board: **This is very bad.** The kids waited as Pavlov wrote more: **I read about these creatures on Wikipedia. These are CARNIVOROUS PIGS! They eat frogs and snakes and grasshoppers and fish and...**Pavlov stopped writing and looked up at them.

"AND WHAT?" the kids all said together.

Pavlov continued to write: **AND PEOPLE. Carnivorous pigs EAT PEOPLE.** The kids all screamed, Ms. Barnyard covered her eyes, and Sadie Orson crawled up into a ball and hid under the seat. In the very back seat the Meaner Beaner chuckled and chuckled. Their trip to New Zoo was being ruined and he was as happy as a live fly on a dead buzzard.

Suddenly, Big Mr. Little reached under his seat, took out a paper bag, and stood up from his seat. He opened the bus door and walked down the steps. The kids were shaking with fright. They did not want their favorite bus driver to be eaten by the Carnivorous Pigs. Big Mr. Little walked through the deep mud towards the squealing pigs, and then he reached into the bag. The kids pressed their noses against the windows. What was in that paper bag? What was Mr. Little doing?

"You little pigs look very hungry," he said. The pigs all nodded their heads. "You little pigs like to eat small children," he said. The pigs all nodded their heads. "Well then," he said, pulling a handful from the paper bag, "perhaps you would like a little snack of THIS today," and the bus driver opened his large hand. Every pig could see what it was, and every pig was horrified at what Mr. Little wanted them to eat. It was BACON. Big Mr. Little wanted the pigs to eat BACON!

The Carnivorous Pigs began squealing louder than ever. The thought of eating their own cousins terrified their pig brains and they stormed through the mud, back into the dark forest.

When every pig was out of sight, Big Mr. Little went to the back bumper of the bus and gave a tremendous heave, and with all of his might he pushed the bus up the hill and out of the mud. The kids all cheered: "YYYEAAAAAHH! Big Mr. Little saved us from the Carnivorous Pigs. Big Mr. Little is the BEST BUS DRIVER in the whole world!"

At the back of the bus the Meaner Beaner frowned. "Rats," he said to himself. "Just when things were getting to be fun."

Big Mr. Little followed the map down Riker's Road and made a left turn onto Pike's Lane." Once again he scratched his head and said to Ms. Barnyard, "This is very strange. Are you sure this is the way to New Zoo?"

"The map is always right, Mr. Little. That's what we learn at school. Trust the map. Trust the map."

Sadie was back in her seat and the kids were once again singing as the yellow bus sped down Pike's Lane. Suddenly the bus entered a long tunnel and they drove and drove in total darkness. The inside of the bus was as black as a skunk hole. Sadie Orson was not happy. "I am worried about this tunnel," she said.

As the yellow bus came out of the tunnel, the road was

becoming skinnier and skinnier. Finally, they stopped. It was a dead end. Big Mr. Little read the sign:

---

**Welcome to the Murky Bog.  BEWARE.**

---

"Oh no!" yelled Stuttering Billy Taberham. "This is M...M...Murky B...B...Bog. This is where the Cyclops lives." All of the kids knew it was true. This was the home of the giant, one-eyed, Murky Bog Cyclops. They all knew that the Murky Bog Cyclops loved children. He wanted to drag them into his home, in the deep, watery Murky Bog.

"Look!" shouted Louie Gomez. "There is something coming out of the bog!" As the kids looked out of the windows, they all screamed at once: "AAAAAAUUUHHH, the Cyclops will drag us into Murky Bog. AAAAAAAAUUUUHHHHHHHHH." Sure enough, rising up from the dark, steamy bog, came the Cyclops, its stiff arms reaching straight out, dripping with black mud, and smelling like an old boot. Slowly, slowly, the one-eyed giant made its way to the bus door. His huge eye looked up, into the faces of the bus riders, and a long, green tongue came out of his mouth. The Cyclops wanted to take the children home. Home to the murky bog. When the Cyclops began rattling the bus door, Sadie Orson screamed: "I hate the Murky Bog. I hate the Murky Bog."

Suddenly, Big Mr. Little jumped up from the driver's seat, opened the bus door and stepped up to the Cyclops and said, "You need to go home. Your mommy is waiting! The bus driver stretched out his huge hands, lifted the Cyclops over his head, and threw the mighty giant back into the bog. Back to his mommy in the murky bog. The kids in the bus once again cheered: "HOOOORAAAAAAAY for Mr. Little, the BEST bus driver in the whole world!" At

the back of the bus the Meaner Beaner grumbled, "Rats! I kind of liked that Cyclops man."

Big Mr. Little turned the bus around and continued to follow the map. "Ms. Barnyard," he said, "are you sure this map is right? I am not so sure that this is the way to New Zoo."

"Maps are never wrong, Mr. Little. Trust the map. Trust the map."

Just as the map directed, the bus made a right turn onto Dark Lane. Big Mr. Little drove and drove until Dark Lane took them into Shady Cave. "Oh no!" screamed Frannie O'Neill. "We have entered Shady Cave, home of the Blood-sucking Bats," and suddenly thousands of the winged mammals were all around the bus, flapping at the windows, scratching the rooftop, gnawing the door handle, trying to find a way into the bus.

Sadie Orson was more worried than ever: "I need my blood!" she cried over and over. "I need my blood!"

Just then, Big Mr. Little got up from his seat and grabbed the lunch bucket under his seat. "Give me your lunch buckets," he said, and all the children—except for one—did as they were told. The bus driver took the lunch buckets in his arms, opened the door, and went out into the black cave. All of a sudden the cave became as quite as a tomb. There was not one screech to be heard. Not one scratch. Not one gnaw. Now, all of the kids were worried about Big Mr. Little. Perhaps the bats had sucked his blood.

The dark bus was silent for fifteen minutes. No one said a word. Even the Meaner Beaner looked a little frightened.

In twenty-two minutes the door of the bus opened. Big Mr. Little stepped in, carrying the lunch buckets. He had no teeth marks on his neck. He looked okay. Big Mr. Little stood at the front of the bus and told them, "Vampire bats are kind little mammals. The mother bats look after their babies very well. The baby bats were hungry and the mother bats only wanted to get them some food. I poured them some milk from your thermos bottles and they brought their babies for a drink. Today all of you helped to feed the vampire bats and they are very happy. They will never forget you. It is now safe to go." Big Mr. Little started the bus and they moved out of the cave. All of the kids waved good-bye to the little vampire bats. All of the kids except the one in the very back seat.

The kids from Brick Street School would never know how, but Big Mr. Little finally got to New Zoo. Years later, the kids would say that this field trip had been the best in the history of Brick Street School. They would always remember the marvelous Carnivorous Pigs, they would remember how Big Mr. Little threw the mighty Cyclops into the Murky Bog, and they would always remember the food they gave to the blood-sucking vampire babies of Shady Cave. It was a truly magical trip.

But the most magical moment of all would come at the zoo. The Meaner Beaner had somehow become lost, and they searched and searched for him. Finally, they found him. No one would ever know how, but the Meaner Beaner had become stuck in the monkey cage. And as all of the kids looked at the cage, with the Meaner standing beside a brown monkey, Billy Taberham would tell the best joke of his life: "I can't tell which one is the m...m...monkey and which one is the M...M...Meaner." And the whole class laughed and laughed. Even Ms. Barnyard. Even Mr. Little.

Even the monkey.

# Chapter Ten

## The Big Game

The people of Tin City could hardly wait for the first Saturday in October. On this day all people, big and small, knew where they would be. On the first Saturday in October, Jimmi Ho's Chinese General Store would be closed, just as every store in Tin City would be closed. On this special Saturday the museum would not be open for business, nor would the marina at Brick Lake, nor would the junkyard, nor would the Laundromat on Hog Street. You could never get your car fixed on the first Saturday in October. Not in Tin City. On this day a big person could never go to Big Jail; a little person could never go to Kids' Jail and a pet could never go to Pets' Jail. You could not get a tattoo, no matter how badly you needed one. You could not get a haircut nor could you get a sore tooth fixed. On the first Saturday in October, every year, Tin City was closed down. This was the day of the Big Game.

Mayor Nancy was the coach of the Tigers—best tackle football team in fifty years. But could they win the Big Game? Could they beat the Badville Badgers—the roughest, toughest, dirtiest tackle football team in Ohio?

On the day before the Big game, a soft breeze rattled the trees along Brick Street and leaves of every color twirled down to the sidewalk. Outside Jimmi Ho's Chinese General Store, Marjorie Kell and her pet monkey, Danny, were eating giant ice cream cones, one strawberry, one butter pecan. Just then, the Meaner Beaner walked up to them, with Rat Zakary riding on his shoulder. "Hey, Meaner," said Marjorie, "are you going to the Big Game tomorrow? Mayor Nancy says that this year's Tin City

Tigers is the best team in fifty years. It is going to be a great game of tackle football."

"TACKLE FOOTBALL IS FOR PINHEADS!" said the Meaner. "I would really like to see those SSSSSTUPID Tigers get beat again this year. That would be very good to see, very good to see."

Marjorie giggled. "The Tigers can't lose!" she said. "This year, they are unbeatable! Besides, Mayor Nancy is the coach and she says that she has a secret weapon this year. A secret weapon! We can't lose!"

Just then, Marjorie and Danny the Monkey turned to look out the front window. As they looked away, the Meaner and Zakary took a big bite from Danny's butter pecan ice cream cone and they darted out the store. As they ran out, Danny squealed and squealed and squealed. Walking home, with ice cream on their faces, the human and the rat laughed and laughed. "That Danny is a very SSSSSTUPID monkey," said the Meaner. "A very SSSSSTUPID monkey." Nyuk, nyuk, nyuk, went the Meaner Beaner. Chidder, chidder, chidder, went Rat Zakary.

From his bedroom window, the Meaner Beaner watched the Brickstreeters go up and down the sidewalk. The kids stopped to talk to each other about the Big Game. They were so excited, so happy—and it gave the Meaner a sharp pain in his behind. The Meaner turned off his bedroom light, but Zakary's fiery red eyes lit up one corner of the room. The Meaner looked deep into the Zakary's red eyes and, suddenly, ZZZZZZZZZAAAAP, an idea shot out of the rat's brain, streaked through the bedroom air, and made its way to the Meaner's brain. An idea that was badder than a dog bite, but more delicious than a stolen bite of ice cream. Bad and delicious—just right for a

Meaner Beaner. Yes, yes, tomorrow would be the BEST
SATURDAY IN THE HISTORY OF TIN CITY. The Tigers
would lose the Big Game. The Meaner Beaner and Rat
Zakary would make sure of that!

Lying on his pillow, the Meaner could see it in his
mind: The unbeatable Tigers would get beat! The big
people of Tin City would be moaning and the little people
would be groaning. The kindergarten kids would be
wailing. Every Tin City monkey would be squealing in
pain, every pig oinking, every mynah bird squawking,
every snake hissing, every dog barking, every emu
blinking, and every cat meowing. Every living thing in Tin
City would feel the deep pain of defeat. Every living thing,
except for two. The boy and the rat from 11 Brick Street,
pals, partners in crime, the 'dastardly duo,' the 'terrible
two,' friends to the end of time. They would be chuckling
and chiddering, chuckling and chiddering. For the rat and
the boy, this would be a beautiful, beautiful thing.

That night, the night before the Big Game, the Meaner
sneaked out of bed and tiptoed to his dark basement. With
every muscle he had, he carried the **Secret Box of No-Good
Dirty Rotten Tricks** up the stairs, outside, and onto his red
wagon. Riding high on the Meaner's shoulder, was Rat
Zakary.

Saying not a word, the 'terrible two' made their way to
Tin City Stadium. The place was as dark and empty as
Mother Hubbard's cupboard. He pulled the wagon into the
open-air stadium, and with only the yellow moon for light,
the Meaner opened the **Secret Box of No-Good Dirty Rotten
Tricks**. He took out everything he would need—everything
he would need to make sure the Tigers would LOSE the
Big Game, everything he would need to RUIN the day for
every living thing in Tin City.

From the box he took one large can of Super Glue. He took out one jar of exploding laughing-gas pellets. He took out two aluminum cans—one full of honey and one full of stinging hornets. He reached way down and took out one pea shooter and one long sleeper dart.

Under the guiding light of the moon, the boy and the rat walked through the stadium, with its steel posts and beams, to a locked wooden door. The sign on the door read:

---

### Equipment Room of Tin City Tigers—Keep Out.

---

Rat Zakary chewed the lock off the door and they went inside. They flicked on a light. The room was filled with football equipment of every kind: whistles, footballs, spiked shoes, helmets, jock straps and uniforms. The Meaner and Zakary shut the door behind them. The 'dirty duo' worked on their capers. They worked long and hard all through the night. Caper after caper after caper. Chuckle after chuckle after chuckle. For them, TOMORROW WOULD BE A WONDROUS DAY!

It was a bright, breezy Saturday as the people and pets of Tin City made their way to the stadium. One by one they filed through the turnstiles and into their seats. The Tiger fans, dressed in orange and black, sat in the EAST side of the stadium. The Badger fans, dressed in dirt brown, sat in the WEST side of the stadium. The Badger fans looked very rough and very tough.

By high noon, the entire stadium was wild with hundreds of cheering fans. The happy people of the EAST side chanted together:

**One two three four**
**Tigers Tigers win some more**

One two three four

For our Tigers we will roar.

And they stood, every Tiger fan on the EAST, and they gave an enormous Tiger RRROOOOOOOOOOAAARRRRR that could be heard all the way to New York City.

Not to be outdone, the not-so-good people of the WEST side chanted together:

Badgers Badgers

We won't fail

Bite those Tigers

On their tails

And then they stood, every Badger fan on the WEST, and they gave an enormous Badger YYYOOOOOOOOOOO that could be heard all the way to Miami, Florida.

Pavlov and all of the Brick Street kids sat together on the EAST side. They were Tiger fans, every one. Just before the game started, Sadie Orson peered through her binoculars at the WEST side. "Oh no!" she said out loud.

"What's the matter?" they all asked.

Still peering through the binoculars, she told them: "The Meaner Beaner and Rat Zakary are sitting with the enemy! They are on the WEST side! They are both dressed in dirt-brown colors and, and, and..."

"And what?" asked Abby Willshire.

"And... the Meaner and Zakary are cheering for the Badgers. THEY ARE CHEERING FOR THE ENEMY!"

Just then, the brainy dog, Pavlov, scribbled something on his chalkboard and he showed them all: **Something rotten will happen today**. And for the first time, all of them worried a little.

Finally, it was game time. The Tin City band came onto the field, along with a singer. It was a very famous singer. "Look!" said Mouse Krause. "It's Jennifer Lopez. She is going to sing the national anthem." The EAST side and the WEST side cheered wildly as Jennifer Lopez stepped up to the microphone and, as the band struck the first note of the Star Spangled Banner, every human and pet in Tin City Stadium stood up fast and straight. But, all at once, a loud RRRRRRRIIIIIIIIIIIIIIIIIIIIIIIIIIIIIIIIIIIIIIIIPPPPPPPPP echoed through the stadium. It was a rip that could be heard all the way to Boston, Massachusetts. It was a rip that came from the EAST side of the stadium. Every Tin City fan put their hands behind them. They could not believe what their hands were feeling.

Their rear ends had been ripped clean off! The rear ends of pants and dresses were stuck to the stadium seats, every one. Annabelle's pet Emu had its rear-end feathers ripped clean off. Sadie Orson's pet gerbil lost it's rear-end fur, and Goose Anderson's pig lost its rear-end hair. The rear end of every human and pet on the EAST side was skinned bare. The Tiger fans knew instantly what had happened. Someone had put Super Glue on their seats. Yes, their rear ends had been Super-glued to the seats of Tin City Stadium! When they turned around, the Badger fans on the WEST side could see two thousand shiny rear ends, and they laughed and laughed and laughed. And laughing loudest of all, were the newest Badger fans, William Joseph Beaner and his little pet rat.

"I am worried about this," said Sadie Orson. "Very worried." Pavlov had some puppy fur ripped from his behind. On his chalkboard, Pavlov wrote them all a message: We must have patience today. Much patience.

When the laughter had settled down, it was time for the kickoff. The great players of the Tin City Tigers were all in a straight line, and when the whistle sounded, they ran all together towards center field. In the middle of the line was the Tiger kicker. As the kicker and the line of Tigers got closer and closer to the ball, the fans of the EAST side began the countdown: TEN, NINE, EIGHT, SEVEN, SIX, FIVE, FOUR, THREE, TWO, ONE— KICKOFF! The foot of the mighty kicker met the football— and, in the second that it did, a tremendous explosion occurred. A cloud of greenish-yellow smoke formed in the air over center field. The fans on both sides of the football field gasped. They could not believe what had happened.

The cloud of greenish-yellow smoke engulfed the Tiger players, and the fans watched in silence to see what would happen next. All at once, the Tiger players began to snicker. Soon, the snickers turned to giggles. And the giggles turned to chuckles. And the chuckles turned to laughter. The Tiger players began laughing and laughing and laughing. They laughed so hard, tears were streaming down their cheeks, and their tummies began to hurt. They fell down laughing, every one of them. The players tried to get up and play football, but they could not. No matter how hard they tried to stop laughing, they could not. Finally, Naj Singh turned to Pavlov and he asked the smart dog: "What happened, Pavlov, what happened?" And Pavlov wrote two words on his slate board: **Laughing Gas.**

The Brickstreeters now understood what had happened. All of the fans on the EAST side understood what had happened. The Tigers had been tricked. Someone had spiked the football with laughing gas pellets—pellets that exploded at the kickoff. Mayor Nancy ran onto the field, complaining to the referees, but it did no good.

The rough and tough Badville fans were now cheering loudly. Sadie Orson again peered into her binoculars and she could see William Joseph Beaner and his rat cheering louder than all of them. Things were going terribly wrong for the Tin City Tigers. Would the best team in fifty years get beat in the Big Game? Would this be the saddest day in the history of Tin City?

The first half of the Big Game went badly for the Tin City Tigers. They had laughed way too much. Their running was not as fast as usual; their throwing was not as far; their catching not as spectacular. At half time, the score was 21-to-7 in favor of the Badville Badgers. It was the worst half-time score in the history of the Big Game.

The half-time show was a blast. At least it was for the rough and tough Badger fans. The entire WEST side was dancing and singing to the music of Jennifer Lopez. The Meaner and Zakary danced the Hoolah Boolah as the crowd cheered them on. They sang their chant over and over: Badgers, Badgers, we won't fail. Bite those Tigers on the Tail. Badgers, Badgers we won't fail. Bite those Tigers on the Tail. The fans of the Badville Badgers were as happy as flies on pies—their team was winning the Big Game. They were beating the unbeatable Tigers.

At half time, the EAST side was quiet. The Tin City fans stayed in their seats as they did not want to get their rear ends sunburned. No one sang to the music of Jennifer Lopez. No one danced. They knew that Pavlov was right: they had to be patient. But it was hard to be patient. Just like Sadie Orson, they worried and worried and worried.

The Tin City Tigers played much better during the second half of the Big Game. Mayor Nancy ran up and down the sidelines, encouraging them and telling them what to do. She was a great coach. At the end of the third quarter, the score was getting closer: 28-to-23 in favor of the Badville Badgers. Now, the Tiger fans were hopeful. They were excited. They now cheered and clapped at every good play. Still, no one on the EAST side stood; every Tin

City fan stayed seated; they did not want to get the bare-bum sunburn.

Early in the last quarter of the game, the Tin City Tigers kicked a three-point field goal and now the game was closer than ever: 28-to-26 in favor of the Badgers. The Tiger fans were more hopeful than ever, but still they worried. And they wondered: Does Mayor Nancy really have a secret weapon? When will she use the secret weapon?

With ten minutes left in the game, Sadie Orson once again peered through her binoculars at the WEST side. She could see Meaner Beaner and Rat Zakary. The Meaner was suddenly doing something very strange. He had a wily smile on his face as he reached down and took something from his duffel bag. What was the Meaner doing? Why was he smiling like that? Sadie was very worried, very worried.

Sadie turned her binoculars to the football game, where the Tin City Tigers were now in control of the game. They were running faster than ever, throwing straight passes, making great, leaping catches, and never missing a tackle.

Sadie turned her binoculars back to the Meaner. What was he doing? What was he up to? Just then, the Meaner took the top off of a jar—and instantly a thousand stinging hornets were released. Like tiny jet planes, the hornets buzzed over the heads of the WEST-side fans and they all screamed in the horrid fear of being stung.

But the stinging hornets did not attack the fans. They flew in a straight line towards the football field. The referee blew the whistle to stop the game. All of the people in the stadium looked up in amazement. Mayor Nancy ran onto the field; she could not believe what she was seeing. A thousand stinging hornets were flying towards the players, and the players began to run for cover. But, strangest of

strange, none of the Badger players was being attacked. Not one Badville player was stung. The stinging hornets went straight for the Tin City players. The hornets buzzed down, down into the football pants, down, down into their football underwear, and down, down into their jock straps. Inside the underwear, inside the jock straps, the hornets began to sting. They stung and stung and stung. The players began howling and screaming. AAAAAHHHHHH.

The howling, screaming Tigers had no choice—they were being badly stung and they had to do it. They had to take off their football pants. They took off their football underwear. They took off their jock straps. Sadie Orson screamed, quickly put down her binoculars, and closed her eyes. Mayor Nancy closed her eyes. A white cat named Cindy Lou covered her eyes. Lindy, the girl gerbil, covered her eyes. Every girl and woman and female pet in Tin City Stadium covered her eyes. On the rough and tough WEST side, the Meaner Beaner laughed and he pointed his finger: "Look at those SSSSSTUPID Tigers. They look like babies in a bathtub." And he laughed and laughed and laughed.

The game had to be stopped. Mayor Nancy understood what had happened, and she did not like it! Someone had put honey inside the underwear and the jock straps of the Tin City Tigers—and stinging hornets love honey! She understood, too, that someone was trying to make the Tigers lose the Big Game. The Super Glue on the seats, the laughing gas football, the honey jock straps and the stinging hornets. Someone was doing rotten capers. She knew she had to do something. Mayor Nancy called a time-out, and she talked to her players. The Tigers listened to every word:

"We have seven minutes left in the Big Game. We can

still win. You have all played hard. You have all played with great courage. But most importantly—you have all PLAYED FAIR. The Tin City Tigers have not lost a tackle football game this year, but we have never cheated. We will not cheat today! We must now go out to the football field and play to win! We must play harder than ever! We must play with more courage than ever! We can still win the Big Game! We can still win the Big Game!"

The players ran to the field. The clock was winding down, only two minutes left, and the Tigers had the ball. It was two minutes in football history that Tin City would never forget. Never. The game began, the ball was snapped, the Tin City quarterback had the ball, and he looked down field. With less than one minute left, he again looked down field and spotted an open man. It was Tommy Choo, best catcher and fastest runner in Tin City. The quarterback threw the ball. It was a perfect pass, and Tommy Choo jumped high in the air and pulled it to his chest. He ran like the wind for the end zone; no one could catch him now. But then it happened—and Sadie Orson saw it all in her binoculars. She saw the Meaner Beaner reach into his duffel bag and pull out his long pea shooter. He loaded the shooter and blew hard.

Through her binoculars, Sadie watched it all. Tommy Choo was struck in the backside by a sleeper dart from the Meaner's pea shooter, he fell to the ground and lost the football to the enemy team. The referee stopped the game and Mayor Nancy ran onto the field. Tommy was on the ground, fast asleep, and he had to be carried to the Tiger dressing room. And now, with only 43 seconds left to play, the Badville Badgers had the ball. The rough and tough fans on the WEST were cheering so loudly they could be heard all the way to San Francisco, and the Meaner

Beaner once again laughed and pointed his finger: "Look at that SSSSSTUPID Tommy Choo. He fell asleep on the job!" Nyuk, nyuk, nyuk, went the Meaner, over and over. Chidder, chidder, chidder, went Rat Zakary.

Then a surprise. Mayor Nancy called a final time-out. She took one of her Tiger players out of the game. The stadium was graveyard quiet as a new player walked onto the field. They squinted their eyes, and Sadie Orson peered through her binoculars.

"Who is it, S..S..Sadie?" asked Billy Taberham. "Who is it?" Everyone was nervous and curious. Why was Mayor Nancy putting a new player on the field with only 43 seconds left in the game? Who was this player?

"I can't tell," said Sadie. In fact, no one in the stadium could recognize the new player, who was dressed in full uniform and full helmet. Still, everyone wondered: Who was under that helmet? Who was wearing those football shoes?

The Brickstreeters all turned to Pavlov. If anyone knew, it would be Pavlov. "Who is it, Pavlov? Who is it?" Pavlov wrote two words on his slate board and he showed them: **Secret Weapon**. Yes, of course, this was Mayor Nancy's secret weapon. Suddenly, they were all excited.

The whistle blew and the ball was hiked to the Badger quarterback. The clock was winding down: 28 seconds left in the game...27, 26, 25. The quarterback looked down field. Great, his man was wide open. He threw the football straight and hard, like a perfect arrow in the air. The WEST stood up and cheered, and the EAST sat and gasped. The clock wound down: 19, 18, 17, 16...

Then it happened.

From the Tin City line, the new player sprang into the air. The fans of Tin City had never seen anything like it. It was a high leap and a lightning catch. A supernatural catch. A magical catch. The new player snatched the ball from the air, stole it from the enemy, and then, like the north wind, ran towards the end zone. The new player darted in and out of the Badger players, causing them to slip and fall, flip and flop, and then, with the grace and speed of a cheetah on the African veldt, sprinted into the end zone for a touchdown. The Tin City Tigers had come back to win the Big Game.

Mayor Nancy's secret weapon had saved the day, and the Tin City fans stood and cheered. They did not care about getting sunburned at all. They jumped and cheered and laughed and hugged. And then, all of the people looked to the end zone. They stood and watched as the new player slowly removed the orange and black helmet. The Brickstreeters knew him instantly. Mayor Nancy's secret weapon was none other than Marjorie Kell's brown monkey. Danny the Monkey raised his hand high into the air and the Tin City fans cheered and cheered.

On Monday morning, two days after the game of tackle football, every person in Tin City bought a newspaper. They wanted to read and read and read about the game they had seen on Saturday. The terrific, unforgettable football game. They read the headline, printed in large, bold letters:

---

### TIGERS WIN BIG GAME:
### SECRET WEAPON SAVES THE DAY.

---

There was only one human in all of Tin City who did not buy a newspaper that day: William Joseph Beaner. Up in his bedroom, the Meaner Beaner looked at Rat Zakary.

"It was a bad Saturday, my little friend, a very bad Saturday. Danny the Monkey is now our mortal enemy. Our mortal enemy! But just wait, Zakary, just wait until next year's Big Game. We will caper them real good. We will caper them real good."

Chidder, chidder, chidder, went Rat Zakary.

# Chapter Eleven

## The Headless Horseman of Tin City

Long, long ago, Tin City had no cars or trucks or motor bikes. No electric lights, no microwave ovens, no flushing toilets. No Twinkies to eat, no televisions to watch, no video games to play.

In the olden days of Tin City, people walked from one place to another, or they rode a horse. They got their water from the well. They took a bath only once a month, wore the same socks all week, and went to church for four hours every Sunday. People helped each other to sew quilts, make jam, and build houses and barns. The people of Tin City were happy and good.

All except one. His name was Peter Vonck, an old geezer who lived in a run-down shack beside the pumpkin field at the edge of town. Peter Vonck helped no one with their quilts or their jam or their houses or their barns. He was mean to everyone. He would use nineteen-letter swear words at the general store; he would kick a friendly dog; he would spit on a little kid.

Then, one Halloween night, some Tin City kids went trick-or-treating, and they decided to knock on the craggy door of Peter Vonck. Peter had no treats for the Halloweeners and he told them all to "Get lost." The kids then followed the golden rule of Halloween: no treat—get tricked. They came back to the geezer's shack and began soaping his windows, egging his front door, and tossing walnuts into his chimney.

As the kids were soaping, egging and tossing, Vonck stormed out of the house like a mad man. His hair was wild, his fists were clenched, and his face was blood-red with anger. The mad man yelled nineteen-letter swear words at the kids. He jumped on his black horse, and he chased them. In his hand was the Beating Stick.

The kids ran for their lives as Peter Vonck rode after them—across the pumpkin field, over the town bridge, down the gravel road, through the cow pasture, and into the forest deep and dark. The kids screamed loudly and they ran fast, but the mad-man screamed louder and charged faster on his black horse. The face of Peter Vonck became redder and redder.

Inside the dark forest, the kids ran and ran and ran. They ran until they could hardly breathe. They did not stop running until they were out of the forest and back in Tin City. They ran home, every one, and did not come out for the rest of the night.

The trick-or-treaters of Tin City would never tell their parents what had happened that night. They would never tell anyone that they had gone to Peter Vonck's shack at the edge of town. They would never tell anyone how the mad horseman had chased them into the dark forest.

The next day was the most horrific in the history of Tin City. The dead body of Peter Vonck was found in the dark forest. His head had been cut off, and the Beating Stick lay on the ground beside the body. Vonck's death would always be a mystery in Tin City. No one would ever know how Peter Vonck had died, or how he had lost his head. His black horse was never seen again.

This all happened on a Halloween night, long, long ago. Still, there were stories—about a mysterious horseman appearing on the pumpkin field at the edge of town. Sometimes on full-moon nights—and almost always on Halloween nights.

The Meaner Beaner made his way down Brick Street with Rat Zakary riding high on his shoulder. The 'gruesome twosome' walked in the direction of Jimmi Ho's Chinese General Store. It was a gray Halloween day with fast-moving, low-flying clouds in the sky. Brown leaves scurried along the sidewalk, and the kids of Brick Street wrapped themselves in long, warm coats. Halloween was the Meaner's favorite—better than Christmas, better than Valentine's Day, better than his own birthday. Tonight, when the harvest moon was full and orange, he and Zakary would caper the littlest trick-or-treaters. They would caper them "real good."

Outside Jimmi Ho's store, the kindergarten kids were talking and laughing and eating giant ice cream cones. They were having such fun! As the Meaner watched them, he got a pain in his behind—HE HATED WHEN THOSE KINDERGARTEN KIDS HAD FUN!

The Meaner stepped up to the kids. He looked down at them, and he used his creepiest voice: "What are you little kids doing?" He glared at the little kids, like a snake glares at mice. The kindergarten kids stopped eating their giant ice cream cones. They all knew the Meaner and Zakary and they were a little afraid. "You kids better watch it," he told them. "When you go out on this Halloween night, you better watch out for the Headless Horseman of Tin City. The man with no head will be on his horse, looking for kids with candy. The Headless Horseman will chase you and steal your candy."

Their knees began to shake. Their ice cream cones began to drip, drip, drip. Every kid in Tin City had heard about the Headless Horseman. Little Jack Fonzio spoke up: "What should we do, Meaner? What should we do?"

In his best creepy whisper, the Meaner told them:

"Listen very carefully. You kids need to stick together tonight. Go trick-or-treating. Get your candy. And then go up to McGuillacutty's pumpkin field at the edge of town. When you get to the pumpkin field, wait for me and Rat Zakary. We will protect you. We will protect you from the Headless Horseman of Tin City. We will not let the Headless Horseman steal your candy. But—you must keep this a secret. Do not tell anyone that you are going to the pumpkin field. Do you understand?"

The kids all nodded their heads. They would keep the secret.

The Meaner and Zakary went away, leaving the kindergarten kids to finish their giant ice cream cones. Now, when the little kids thought about the Headless Horseman of Tin City, they were not afraid. They felt safe. Tonight they would go trick-or-treating, and then they would go the pumpkin field. They would tell no one. The Meaner Beaner and Rat Zakary would protect them.

Halloween night was cool. The full moon spied on all the trick-or-treaters as they made their way from house to house. The orange moon watched them all: Abby Willshire and Annabelle Jefferson as Purple People Eaters; Benny Lee as the dreaded Murky Bog Cyclops; Naj Singh as the Night Scratcher; stuttering Billy Taberham as a slimy-green g...g...ghoul; Sadie Orson, the pink, winged fairy; Goose Anderson, the evil dungeon master; Mouse Krause, the sleek, black, Cat Woman; Frannie O'Neill, an evil, green leprechaun; Julie Fonzio and Marjorie Kell, Carnivorous Pigs, snorting and grunting as they walked down the street; and Pavlov, the haunting ghost-dog raised from its grave in Pet Cemetery.

And far down Brick Street, the orange moon spotted something else. It was a menacing creature with slicked-back hair, red eyes, and sharp white fangs. The creature was neatly dressed in a white shirt, dark pants and dinner jacket, and a black cape that sailed back as he walked along. The creature pulled a wagon, with four high racks all around. On the creature's shoulder rode a winged, blood-sucking mammal. The moon knew these tricksters: It was the Meaner Beaner as Count Dracula and Rat Zakary as his vampire bat.

And then came the littlest creatures of Tin City. In masks and costumes of every kind, the kindergarten kids trudged down Brick Street, going house to house, filling their Halloween bags with treats and sweets: Nutty Fruit Gobblers, Electric Choco-berries, Lemon Frazoos, Gloopy Pops, Gummy Reptiles, Red Hot Tongue Blasters, strawberry jaw breakers, licorice Twizzlers, milk chocolates wrapped in foil, sour gumballs, bags of potato chips and cans of pop. They knocked on the doors, filled their bags—and they stuck together, like one big family. They tried their best to be strong and brave—but they held on to their bags of candy very tightly. They watched every tree, every bush, every stone. They watched for the Headless Horseman of Tin City.

When their bags were heavy with treats, and when the time was nearly midnight, the little kids made their way to the pumpkin field at the edge of town. Bravely, silently, they walked up Brick Street, through the cow pasture, down the gravel road, and over the town bridge. And the orange moon watched them.

When the kids reached the field at the edge of town, they saw the dark shape of a vampire sitting on a pumpkin. The kids stopped and stared. "I think it's the Meaner Beaner," said little Jack Fonzio, and they walked closer to the vampire. They spotted the Meaner's red wagon.

"Good even-ing, leettle cheeldren," said the Meaner, sounding like Count Dracula himself. "I haf been vaiting for you." The Meaner looked at their huge bags of delicious candy. "You leettle cheeldren do not need to be afraid. I vill pro-teck you."

"Where is Rat Zakary?" asked little Todd Orson.

The Meaner answered in a whispery vampire voice: "Rat Zakary cood not come out thees even-ing. Him did not vant to be eaten by a Hallo-veen owl. Hallo-veen nights are very dangerous for no-tailed leettle rats."

The kindergarten kids came closer to the vampire. "How will you protect us?" asked little Eddie Willshire. "How will you protect us from the Headless Horseman of Tin City?"

The suspicious moon watched all of them as the vampire talked to the small monsters in the pumpkin field at the edge of town. And the moon heard the vampire tell the children to set their bags of candy on the ground. The moon watched the vampire as he gave each of them a pumpkin. The vampire told the little monsters that these were magic pumpkins. As long as they held on to these pumpkins, they would not be bothered by the bad things of Halloween night—not by a goblin, nor a ghost, nor ghoul, nor a zombie, nor a warlock, nor a toothless witch. They would not be bothered by the Headless Horseman of Tin City. The moon heard the vampire's words very clearly: "Hold on tight to dees magic pump-keens and you vill be safe. Vut-ever you do, do not drop the magic pump-keens." The kids set their bags of candy on the ground and picked up their magic pumpkins.

Then, very suddenly, very horridly, they heard something.

It was an ear-piercing, high-pitched cry—like the wail of a little pig, whose tail was stuck in the fence. But they all knew this was no little pig. The kids looked into the blackness beyond the pumpkin field, and to their horror, they could see two fiery-red eyeballs in the night.

The kindergarten kids screamed, every one of them: AAAAUUUGHHHHHHH, and little Jack Fonzio shouted for all he was worth: "IT'S THE HEADLESS HORSEMAN OF TIN CITY. HOLD ON TO YOUR PUMPKINS. AND, RUN."

And they ran. They ran for their lives. Holding on to their safety pumpkins, the kids ran across the field, over the town bridge, down the gravel road and into the dark forest. They ran through the forest, back to Tin City, and into their own home-sweet-homes.

The Meaner Beaner took off his vampire mask and he laughed. He looked once again at the fiery red eyes in the distance, and once again he laughed. He laughed and laughed and laughed. And then he yelled out: "Zakary, you were sooooooo good! You were sooooooo perfect! Your little red eyes scared those little SSSSSTUPID kindergarten kids. Look, little buddy, look at all that candy they left us! We will be eating candy for a year! Two years! Three years! This is the BEST HALLOWEEN IN THE HISTORY OF TIN CITY." And the Meaner chuckled his Meaner chuckle over and over and over: Nyuk, nyuk, nyuk. Nyuk, nyuk, nyuk. Nyuk, nyuk, nyuk. Nyuk, nyuk, nyuk. Nyuk, nyuk, nyuk. Nyuk, nyuk, nyuk.

The fiery red eyes came closer and closer, but there was no sound. Not one sound did he hear from his little buddy. Not one squeak. Not one chidder. The Meaner stopped his chuckling and squinted his eyes. He could see that the red eyes were high in the air. Higher than Rat Zakary.

Something was not right.

Closer and closer came the red eyes, and the Meaner's black heart began to thump. Just then, the Meaner felt something tugging at his pant leg. He looked down and, in the dim shadows, he could see his little buddy, Rat Zakary.

It came out into the pumpkin field—a dark figure on a magnificent black horse. The Halloween moon shone down on the caped creature as he sat in his saddle, stone silent, facing the two criminals. The Meaner's knees were knocking and Zakary's whiskers were twittering. Now, it was very clear to Zakary and to Meaner: THE CREATURE WAS HEADLESS.

Well, almost headless. In truth, the creature on the horse WAS CARRYING HIS OWN HEAD. HIS OWN CHOPPED-OFF HEAD WITH ITS TWO FIREY RED EYES. In his other hand was an old hickory stick—the Beating Stick!

All at once, they ran. The boy and the rat ran for their lives. They sped across the field, over the bridge, down the gravel road and into a forest as dark as a shoe box. Out of breath, they stopped. They turned, looked back and, as the moon peered down at them, they listened. The forest was like an ancient tomb, all quiet except for the small chattering sounds made by teeth—by a boy's teeth, by a rat's teeth.

Suddenly, more sounds came from the empty forest behind them. Snapping twigs, crackling leaves, thumping earth. In the distance, between the trees, they saw the red eyes coming closer, closer, closer.

The Meaner and Zakary ran to the edge of the forest and, once again, they turned. They looked back in horror. The horseman was on a hill. All at once the black horse reared up and, in one frightful second, the head, with its red eyes, came at the boy and the rat. It came at them as a whirling ball of fire.

For the second time in history the trick-or-treaters of Tin City would never tell their parents what had happened that night. The kindergarten kids would never tell anyone that they had gone to the pumpkin field at the edge of town. They would never tell anyone that they had seen the fiery-red eyes of the Headless Horseman.

William Joseph Beaner would never breathe one word of this Halloween night. Rat Zakary would never squeak one word of this. They did not want people to know that they had run away from the Horseman. They did not want people to know that they were afraid. They did not want people to know that their rear-ends had been burned red by the fiery pumpkin. They would never tell.

Years later, when the Meaner Beaner turned sixteen years old, his mother had a talk with him. She told him of a family secret—a secret he must never tell anyone. She told him that Peter Vonck—the old man who was thought to be the Headless Horseman of Tin City—was the Meaner's great grandfather. The mean old man with the Beating Stick was his own great grandfather.

The Meaner had to promise his mother that he would never tell anyone this terrible, terrible secret. He promised never to tell. Never, never, never.

The next day, at Tin City High School, the Meaner Beaner    told    everyone    the    wonderful    news.

# Chapter Twelve

## The Meaner Beaner Steals Christmas

On December 18 Brick Street was a canvas of white diamond snow. On their way to school the Brick Street kids made goose tracks on the sidewalk and snow angels on the hills. They whipped snowballs at Marjorie Kell's snowman. They loved this crispy-white day!

The Meaner hated days like this. He hated when other kids had winter-fun.

On the way to school the Meaner met Sadie Orson, the worry wart, and her kindergarten brother, Todd. "Hi, Meaner," said Sadie. "Great day, hey? There's absolutely nothing to worry about on a day like this."

"A TERRIBLE day!" growled the Meaner.

"But Christmas is almost here, Meaner!"

"So what?" said the Meaner. He then stared his long mean stare at Sadie's little brother. "That kid looks like a monkey!"

Little Todd's lip began to quiver and he snuggled closer to big sister. Sadie stepped right up to the Meaner: "Leave him alone!" She then turned to the little brother and whispered, "It's okay, Todd, it's just the Meaner Beaner...He likes to act mean, but he won't hurt you. Frannie O'Neill says he was born that way. She said he was hatched from an egg. A very rotten egg!"

Sadie took her brother's hand. "See you, Meaner," she said. The Meaner gave them the famous Meaner chuckle, Nyuk, nyuk, nyuk, and walked on.

By the time school was over, the snow on Brick Street was knee high and soft as cotton. Benny Lee ran all the way home. He had to help Mom put up the Christmas lights.

Benny and his Mama Lee worked for hours in the still, cold night. Up the side of the house, across the eave trough, around the bay window, over the door, and around and around the bird house pole. At 8:00 o'clock Benny flicked on the blue lights.

Benny and his mom stood on the sidewalk, and for a long time they watched their brilliant lights. To Benny his house was a ship, a big white ship, sailing on an ocean of blue lights. At this moment Benny Lee was the proudest boy in the whole world.

This Christmas the Fonzios went red and green. All around the garage door, up the east side of the house, down the west side. When the lights were flicked on, little Jack Fonzio stood, amazed. "They look like jelly beans," he said to sister Julie. "Jelly beans, all strawberry and lime."

"Yummy," said Julie, "strawberry and lime are the best jelly beans of all." At this moment Jack and Julie Fonzio thought they had the most amazing lights in the entire universe.

The Taberhams draped blinking white lights on all of their bushes and evergreen trees. On and off and on and off and on and off. "They will be our Christmas f...f...f...fireflies," said stuttering Billy. "They are the most amazing lights on B...B...Brick Street."

The house where Pavlov and his pet boy, Jeremy, lived was red brick and decorated with purple lights. But in the center of the snow-covered lawn was the best decoration of all—a giant, wooden bone, draped with a thousand purple lights. Pavlov and Jeremy had worked all day, stringing lights around the house and on the giant bone. Pavlov was now the happiest dog on Brick Street.

The Andersons went with red lights and a blinking star

on the roof. "Gosh," said Goose Anderson, "this is the most amazing place in all of Tin City. I bet even William Joseph Meaner Beaner would love it!"

The Meaner Beaner walked east on Brick Street. He stopped to notice Benny Lee's sea of blue lights. "SSSSSTINKS," said the Meaner.

He walked by Fonzio's red and green jelly bean lights. "ROTTEN JELLY BEANS," said the Meaner.

He trudged by the Taberhams, where the white lights blinked, blinked, blinked like a thousand Christmas f...f...fireflies. "SSSSSTUPID," said the Meaner.

He made his way to Goose Anderson's house. He noticed their red lights and blinking star on the roof. "MAKES ME SSSSSICK," said the Meaner.

He stopped on the sidewalk in front of Pavlov's red brick house. He looked at all the purple lights and at the giant wooden bone in the front yard. "PURPLE IS FOR PINHEADS," he grumped to himself.

By 10:00 o'clock the winter sky was black as soot, but Brick Street was a wonderland of lights. Some of the lights blinked and some of them did not, but all of them lit up Brick Street like a giant Christmas tree. All the kids on the sidewalk thought that their street must surely be the most amazing place on the planet, Earth.

Not William Joseph Beaner. Back in his own cozy bedroom the Meaner groused about Christmas with his one true friend, Rat Zakary. "Those Brickstreeters think they are so fancy," said the Meaner. They are outside laughing and holding hands and looking googly-eyed at those SSSSSTUPID lights. "I HATE IT WHEN THOSE GOODIE-GOODIES HAVE SO MUCH FUN!"

Zakary the rat looked up from his wire cage, with his eyes as red as blood. When Zakary smiled, his teeth glimmered like a fish knife and the fur on his back stood straight up. The Meaner stared into Zakary's red eyes. He stared deeper and deeper and deeper—and then, like magic, the Meaner was struck in the brain with a wonderful caper. A terribly terrific, wonderfully irresponsible caper. The best dirty deed he could ever imagine. He would STEAL Christmas on Brick Street. Nyuk, nyuk, nyuk, went the Meaner. Chidder, chidder, chidder, went Rat Zakary.

At 11:00 p.m. on December 19 the Meaner sneaked out of bed, quiet as the night, put on a snowsuit over his pajamas, pulled on his green and purple woolen mittens, and jumped out his bedroom window. His red wagon was waiting in the garage, with four high racks all around, ready for the night. In the wagon, was his partner in crime, Rat Zakary, with his tiny earmuffs, tiny scarf, and tiny mittens of wool.

In front of Benny Lee's house the Meaner looked left, he looked right, he looked front and behind. Nobody around. His boots scarcely made a sound as he sneaked up to the house and began the dirty deed. One by one he unscrewed the blue lights and dropped them into his red wagon. When he was done, the Meaner turned and snickered his meanest snicker. "I sunk that ship," he smirked to himself. Chidder, chidder, chidder, went Rat Zakary.

The Meaner pulled his wagon up to the Fonzio's garage. He looked left and right and front and behind. Nobody around. In fifteen minutes all of Fonzio's red and green jelly bean lights were in the red wagon. The Meaner grinned his meanest grin. We ate those jelly beans," he muttered to his furry friend.

Nobody around at the Taberhams. Now it was

Zakary's turn. With his sharp teeth Zakary plucked the blinking white lights from the bushes and evergreens and plopped them into the wagon. The Meaner chuckled his meanest chuckle and mumbled to himself, "The Christmas fireflies have been snatched by a rat!"

In ten minutes the Zakary was on Goose Anderson's rooftop, creeping along, silent as the snow. The rat unlit the star and unscrewed every red light around the house. The Meaner laughed and laughed. "They don't call me the Meaner Beaner for nothing," he said to Zakary.

The Meaner and Zakary crept along the snow in front of Pavlov's house. Together they unscrewed every purple light from the red brick house and kicked over the giant wooden bone in the front yard. When the bone fell over in the snow, the 'dastardly duo' laughed and chiddered, laughed and chiddered.

Their next stop was 75 Brick, the Sledgehammer house. The Meaner swallowed hard as he sneaked up to the front porch. Bernice Sledgehammer lived here—Freddy Sledgehammer's favorite aunt. Even at Christmas time Freddy liked to scare kids with his big, hard fist—he called it the Christmas Sledgehammer. The Meaner kind of liked Freddy, but the thrill was too much. The wily Meaner unscrewed Bernice Sledgehammer's lights and piled them on his wagon.

By midnight the Meaner and Zakary were nearly done. With Rat Zakary riding on top of all the lights, the Meaner pulled the loaded wagon up to his own house and, to make the crime perfect, unscrewed the lights his mom and dad had put up just last night. He then turned and gave Brick Street one last look. It was a wonderland no more. It was cold and empty and blacker than the blackest chalkboard. It was like a graveyard on Halloween night. At this moment William Joseph Beaner was the happiest kid on Brick Street...maybe the entire universe. "Merry Christmas, Brickstreeters, Merry Christmas." Nyuk, nyuk, nyuk, he sniggered. Chidder, chidder, chidder, went Rat Zakary.

December 20 was a dark day for Brick Street. At least it was a dark night. When Benny Lee flicked on the switch, there was no sea of blue lights.

When Julie Fonzio flicked on the switch, no red and green jelly bean lights.

When Billy Taberham flicked on the switch, no blinking Christmas f...f...fireflies.

When Goose Anderson flicked on the switch, no star, no red lights.

When Pavlov and Jeremy flicked on the switch, no purple lights, no giant bone in the front yard.

A hundred people came out of their homes. They could not understand this evil mystery. "Who would have done this?" cried little Sadie Orson. "Some bad-hearted creature has come from outer space and ruined our Christmas. I am so worried, so worried."

The Brickstreeters, big and little, walked along the dark street. They had lumps in their throats. They had a sick feeling deep in their tummies. With Rat Zakary perched on his shoulder, the Meaner Beaner also walked the street, trying hard not to smile. He had a mean feeling deep down in his tummy. And he liked it. For Meaner and Zakary, this was going to be the best Christmas ever!

Christmas inched closer, day by day. On December 23 every Brick Street kid was at the park. The warm winter sun made the snow wet and heavy—perfect for a snow fort. The Meaner Beaner strolled into the park, where the kids worked like a colony of busy ants, rolling and lifting and carrying huge snowballs. On the Meaner's shoulder, warm as brown toast in his rat-size parka, his rat-size woolen scarf, his miniature snow-hat and tiny claw warmers, was Rat Zakary.

"Hey Meaner," yelled Annabelle Jefferson, "come on, all the Brickstreeters are here.  We're making the biggest snow fort in the history of Brick Street Park. It's going to be as big as the Titanic."

"Snow forts are for pinheads," the Meaner yelled back. He didn't understand how the Brickstreeters could be so happy, so excited. He and Zakary had worked overtime to steal their Christmas. He kicked the snow, grumbled, and turned to walk away.

But a very BIG, very TOUGH, very BALD-HEADED teenager blocked his way. "Oh, hi, Freddy," said the Meaner, nice as cherry pie.

Freddy Sledgehammer glared down at the Meaner Beaner.  As every kid knew, this guy was bad news, creepy, much meaner than the Meaner. "I have a present for you, Beanbag," said Freddy. His voice was as hard as rusty nails. He reached into his pocket and pulled out something that was green and purple and woolen.

"Hey, Freddy, th...th...that's my glove.  I lost it. Th...th...thanks for finding it." Meaner Beaner began to sweat. Rat Zakary began to sweat.

Freddy Sledgehammer was not smiling. He held the glove in front of Meaner's nose. "I found this beside my Aunt Bernice's garage, Beanbag. RIGHT WHERE HER CHRISTMAS LIGHTS USED TO BE!"

The Brick Street kids left the snow fort and gathered round. They stood in silence. The Meaner was shaking in his boots. Freddy Sledgehammer snarled his dirtiest snarl and showed Meaner his stone-hard fist. He said, "You are the NO-GOOD RAT-FINK who stole my aunt's Christmas. My FAVORITE aunt's Christmas!"

Every eye was on Meaner Beaner. "N...n...n...n...no," he stammered.

"YES!" Freddy yelled. He moved close to the Meaner. Nose to nose. "Do you know what Freddy Sledgehammer does to no-good RAT-FINKS?" Meaner shook his head. He could not talk. Freddy continued: "He hammers them! He SLEDGEHAMMERS them!" Every Brick Street kid could hear the Meaner's teeth chattering.

"Wait!" a small voice spoke. All eyes turned. It was little Benny Lee.

Freddy turned around and scowled at Benny Lee. "Stay out of this, pipsqueak."

Another small voice piped up. "Leave the Meaner alone." It was Julie Fonzio.

"This little rat-fink stole my aunt's lights," Freddy said. "He stole your lights. He ruined Christmas at my aunt's house. He ruined Christmas at your house. Now he is going to get sledgehammered."

"No!" said another small voice. "Just go away! Leave him alone!"

Freddy glared at all of them. "You go away! All of you! OR I WILL SLEDGEHAMMER ALL OF YOU!" He showed them the big fist, the Screaming Sledgehammer.

Mouse Krause, littlest kid in the park, stepped forward. Eye to eye with the mighty Freddy. "Maybe you can sledgehammer me, Freddy...Maybe you can sledgehammer four of us...or six of us...But you can't sledgehammer all of us. There's too many of us."

Suddenly, the air was heavy with silence—and for the first time ever, the mighty Freddy felt an ounce of fear.

"But this kid is a rat-fink! A sneaky rat-fink! A rat-fink who steals Christmas! Kids like that deserve the Screaming Sledgehammer."

Louie Gomez rolled across the snow on his wheelchair: "Nobody deserves the Screaming Sledgehammer, Freddy."

"But that rat-fink took our lights...He stole our Christmas!"

"Not for me," Louie said. "The Meaner didn't steal Christmas for me. Maybe he took my lights, maybe he didn't, I don't really know. But he can't steal my Christmas...not if I don't want him to. My mom says that Christmas shines with a light of its own...and nobody can put that light out...not if we don't want them to."

Freddy turned and walked away from the kids. When he made it all the way to the teeter-totter, he turned and yelled to them: "But he's a Christmas stealer! He's a rat-fink!"

Louie cupped his hands and yelled back: "Maybe he is a rat-fink, Freddy...but he's still a Brickstreeter. He is still our friend. And we all stick up for a Brickstreeter. We stick up for a friend." Louie caught his breath, again cupped his hands and yelled: "That's what Christmas is about, Freddy. It's not the lights. It's sticking up for each other."

"Ah, you shrimps are all crazy," Freddy yelled back and walked away.

The kids all watched the Meaner Beaner. He hung his head and walked towards his home. "Hey, Meaner," Sadie Orson yelled. "We're going for a night skate at the park after supper. Why don't you come?"

"Nah," said the Meaner, "I've got to get my wagon oiled up. I've got a lot of work to do tonight."

The Meaner walked along Brick Street as the kids watched him in silence. When he was far down the sidewalk, he whispered to Zakary, "No more dirty tricks this Christmas." He then snickered to himself and smiled his wily smile. "But I can hardly wait for Easter!"

Chidder, chidder, chidder, went Rat Zakary.

## THE END—OR IS IT?

ISBN 142511827-5